Notes from the Mistress

Love in Black and White

ALICIA HILAIRE

Copyright cover art images and use licenses were secured through

Shutterstock and 123rf.

Portions of this book are works of non-fiction. Certain names and identifying characteristics have been used or changed as appropriate.

Some portions of this book are works of fiction. Any reference to historical events, real people, or real places are used fictitiously. Other names, characters, places, and events are products of the author's imagination, and any resemblances to actual events or places or persons living, or dead are entirely coincidental.

ISBN 978-0-578-67059-1 (paperback)

Library of Congress control number: TXu002190810

Hilaire, Alicia. Notes from the Mistress. – 1st ed.

Publisher: Hilaire Wellness & Beauty Clinics INC

Editor: Kelly Cook

Editor: Derek Nolan

Illustration, design, cover design, titles by Garrett Cook & Kelly Cook

Dedicated To:

My loving husband, Frantz, and

our beautiful children

Contents

Foreword

Notes from the Mistress is the sequel of the debut novel *Sydney's Bleu*. This piece of literature is the response to questions that most people had after reading the first novel about Sydney's journey. There was an influx of phone calls and emails from friends and family asking questions like; "What happened with Mr. Christophe? Did Sydney marry Christophe? Did they stay in Haiti? What happened next?" That's when the inspiration to tell this story ignited. The goal was to create a story inspired by the experience of marriage, which is a very delicate topic. This story reveals how two people from different backgrounds and cultural experiences come together and create their journey called love. Every marriage is different. The complexities that occur within matrimonial relationships can be stories all on their own. Sydney's marriage was no exception. It was filled with enough emotional, spiritual, and physical dynamics to warrant a separate novel. The drama of *Sydney's Bleu* and the challenges of life after trauma deserved two separate homes.

Notes from the Mistress, like *Sydney's Bleu,* is a collection of short stories. In this novel, Sydney is a little bit older and perhaps more mature. She's still very adventurous, yet she tries to make better decisions while standing firm on God's word. The short stories are primarily about Sydney and Christophe's lives. It's the backstory of their relationship, the challenges within their marriage, and their journey to happily ever after.

The significance of the story is tied to the deep history of the main characters, their unique personality traits, and the undercurrent of a personified mistress called music. Sydney and Christophe both are interesting characters and have a unique story. The history of Christophe's parents is introduced in this collection. This story captures a love affair between a man and a woman from two different walks of life. The Notes at the beginning of each chapter are from the perspective of the music. The art form played an instrumental role in their lives to the extent that it had a distinct voice, a distinct presence, and an undeniable positioning throughout their relationship.

The story peeks into Christophe's parents' journey from Haiti to the United States and uncovers Christophe's love of music. His wife Sydney is the love of his life, but he is terribly addicted to music to the point that he often uses song lyrics to express his feelings. He communicates well, however, when it comes to his feelings; he can easily find a song that captures the essence of the moment.

Their relationship is filled with many international travel experiences, some together and some apart. During a visit to Haiti, Christophe introduces Sydney to his mother's homeland. They discover a rich history and develop a passion for the forgotten village from where his mother migrated. Sydney and Christophe also travel to France. While there, they explore different regions, meet interesting people, and enjoy wine excursions as they rekindle their marriage.

Acknowledgments

A special "thank you" goes out to my loving husband, my muse. Thanks for allowing me the time I needed to express my colorful imagination about you and our life together. To be an indie author, in this literary piece, my aim was to write a beautiful and heartfelt novel. Although it was a long journey, the drama within *Sydney's Bleu* was easy to write about. Conversely, to write a "love story" was a bit more challenging. Reading between the lines is unnecessary; it's all here. In this novel, I tried to provide clear depictions of our travels abroad. The time spent in various parts of France and Haiti provided a beautiful backdrop for many of the themes described in this book. Thank you for your love and support on this journey. I hope you enjoy reading this novel as much as I enjoyed writing it.

Thank you to my amazing children. I am so proud of you all. I gave you all to God and I trust that He will have his way in all of your lives. Thanks, Mom, for allowing me to express my thoughts and memories about our family. You are a good mother and a true friend. Your support through all the challenges has helped me to become a better person.

To my forever friends, I will always have love and respect for you. To my extended family and friends, thank you for your encouragement and support. To my blood sisters (Andrea, Latasha, and Alexis) and my spiritual sisters, I send many thanks and wish you all the best. Thank you for all the prayers and great conversations.

To my brothers, I love you and I hope that you will find true love and I hope you know that you deserve love, honor, and respect. You are kings, descendants from the Most High God.

To all the women who read this novel, my heart goes out to you all. Married, single, or divorced, all I can say is trust the power of God to work a miracle in your life, your relationships and in your marriage. With Him, all things are possible.

Thank you to my friend and editor, Kelly. You made this project something that I am truly proud of. I could not complete this art piece without your creative talents. Because of you and our friendship, I felt comfortable sharing the story with you, asking silly questions, and becoming vulnerable with the content of the story. Because of you, I was able to laugh at my ideas that were ridiculous but also correct ideas so that they came across in the right context for which I had intended. After months of working through this piece, we both were able to sign off, seal and deliver a beautiful love story. I am grateful for you and Garret. You both are so talented. I appreciate your time and creativity.

Thank you to the Nolan family. I am grateful to have your friendship and support. Derek, thanks for stepping in and working on this project. Your contributions are greatly appreciated. You are so talented. Keep up the good work.

ᘉ 1 ᘉ

Chapter 1: New Beginnings

The Lord's Prayer in French, Notre Père (Our Father):

Notre Père, qui es aux cieux,

Que ton nom soit sanctifié,

Que ton règne vienne,

Que ta volonté soit faite sur la terre comme au ciel.

Donne-nous aujourd'hui notre pain de ce jour.

Pardonne-nous nos offenses.

Comme nous pardonnons aussi à ceux qui nous ont

offensés.

Et ne nous soumets pas à la tentation,

mais délivre-nous du mal,

car c'est à toi qu'appartiennent le règne,

la puissance et la gloire, aux siècles des siècles.

Amen.

The 1st Note:

Truly hopeful, and full of excitement were the sentiments that she felt as she entered 2020. Somehow, she survived and beat the odds, which were heavily stacked against her. It would be unfair to say that arriving at her current state of being was an easy task because it was not. Soul searching, introspection, and of course listening to me allowed her to catapult into a newfound awareness and purpose of her existence. I had a peripheral existence in her life growing up. I have always been there, in the background. I helped to heal her wounds, mend her broken heart, celebrate her joys and bring her closer to God. She understood me, I understood her.

To develop and grow to the point where she is today, it was necessary to revisit some events from her past. She had to evaluate how her own decisions left a lasting impact on her life. She admitted that she had made some irresponsible choices for which she clearly had to suffer the consequences. She realized that each time she made a foolish choice, she never truly considered how her actions would impact her family or herself. While living in the moment and living a carefree life, she only considered her selfish desires to have fun. She was spiritually bankrupt and immature, therefore she engaged in many worldly pleasures, not knowing how her childish ways would cause an undesirable amount of regret and dissatisfaction with life.

So, fast-forwarding to the present, how did she arrive at this current state of being, which included the ever-elusive happiness? What was the secret to obtaining peace, joy, and contentment within her? How did she, Sydney Ann Marie, come to a place of acceptance, where she successfully plays the cards that life has dealt her? How did she move forward in becoming more positive and optimistic? I can easily describe Sydney's journey. I was there in the depths of her mind. I mirrored the course of her life through song, like in the words from "Clean Up What I Messed Up" by the Canton Spirituals. This song perfectly describes Sydney's earlier days of continued restarts after life's challenges. "Endow Me" by the Clark Sisters, describes her deep desire to have a relationship with God; for Him to move in her life and use her for His will. "My Heart

Has Been Restored," by Maurette Brown Clark, speaks her feelings about returning to a relationship with God. It acknowledges moments of unbelief and wavering faith. However, it also explains God's changing power in her and how she trusts again through renewed faith. "I Told The Storm" by Greg O'Quin 'N Joyful Noize, not only acknowledges that there will be challenges in life; it also encourages her to fight through those challenges with faith. Then finally, some of my most tender and eloquent words were spoken with, "You Bring Me Joy" by Anita Baker. I dove into the abyss of her feelings, in a love letter sort of way, for Christophe. My dear Christophe, one of my many conquests. These songs are the score to scenes from Sydney's life. The lyrics embody such depth and emotion, while their melodies offer relief for the heart and soul.

This is how Sydney tells the journey, in her own words:

The course of my life drastically changed after having a nervous breakdown and I was admitted into Summit Ridge, a mental health facility located in northwest Georgia. While lying unconscious in the hospital's intensive care unit, I saw my life flash before my eyes as the Gwinnet County paramedics pumped my stomach and battled to resuscitate my lifeless body. What may have appeared to be a suicide attempt was just my way of expressing that I was extremely overwhelmed. I didn't truly want to kill myself and banish from the earth; I just wanted a break away from it all. My soul was in need of a time-out. I had been listening to somber music thinking about how life had taken its toll on me. The pressures from society to have a certain status and to be a perfect mother were heavy burdens to bear. Financial pressures and the pressure I felt of being a single woman trying to provide for my children were both taxing issues. I had the pressure of not fitting in and always feeling alone. Being an introvert and having a personality that is frequently misunderstood stifled my ability to cultivate any true friendships. I, therefore, had no one to talk to and just being alive felt overwhelming.

  I had to undergo daily sessions of counseling and talk therapy while I was hospitalized in order to become mentally healthy and begin the process of recovery. The experienced psychologists were eager to include anti-depressants with my treatment plan and promised me that the drugs were not addictive. I followed the medical professional's instructions although my body had an adverse reaction to the various mind-altering prescriptions. The first anti-depressant, Paxil, simply dried my tear ducts, which curbed all my emotions. The uncontrollable spells of crying had stopped but I know the meds increased my negative thoughts, so the doctors switched me over to Zoloft. With Zoloft, I could not sleep at night; the medication or the dosage caused my body to tremble all day and throughout the night. That drug felt more like a tranquilizer. Instead of helping me get well, I felt mentally impaired. Shaky, like a wet dog standing outside during a hailstorm, is how that drug made my body feel. For at least two weeks, I did not know who I was. The doctor gave me Celexa after no success with the first two prescriptions. While taking Celexa, my body was immune to all drama. For example, if my children were crying, the meds made me laugh and I would ignore their loud weeping. If something terrible was happening, I would laugh at the situation as if it were a joke. While taking the medications, there was always a lack of sensation or I felt numb and loopy. It was as if I was detached from any true emotions, or my natural emotion for each given situation was a mismatch.

Although it was a struggle, I was determined to have a good quality of life. I did not want to rely on daily medications; instead, I began to research natural ways to deal with my health issues. I chose alternative coping methods to fight against depression. I refused to allow what doctors call a "mental disease" to slow me down or disable me.

The first major step I had to take towards gaining a better life was to be honest with myself. It was necessary to hold myself accountable for my wrongs. I had to accept the bad choices that I made, and I also had to accept the blame. No more lying to myself about my wrongdoings. No more blaming my parents or blaming the men of my past for my unhappiness. I had made numerous thoughtless decisions and I was the person responsible for my success or misfortune; no one else but the woman reflected in the mirror.

The second step I had to take was to forgive myself and forgive others for the pain of my past. I forgave myself for not always putting God first and for making reckless decisions. I had to forgive others for not giving me the love that I needed. I forgave my parents for not providing adequate guidance during my childhood and adolescent years; given their individual circumstances, I acknowledged that they did the best parenting that they could do. I forgave the men from my past relationships for misleading me and not having my best interest at heart. The most difficult thing I had to do was to forgive myself for allowing the continuous cycles of abuse, which was a faulty attempt to gain love.

The third step and most important step for me to get well was to try and understand the meaning of it all. What was the underlying purpose of all the events and the people who played key roles in my life? What was the grand scheme of it all, and why me? Well, simply put, God had already preordained my destiny. The Heavenly Father knew that I would be a perfect example to fulfill His mission. God knew that he could use me for His purpose. He allowed every event of my life and he saw that those events were fitting for my personal testimony. God gave me a daring and adventurous personality because He knew that I would step out on a limb and take a leap for Him to get the glory. The Heavenly Father used me just like he used His Son and He uses all of us, for His purpose. I was made to serve the sovereign God, but it took a while for me to figure it out.

As a young child, when I begged and pleaded with Grandma Nadeya about joining God's army, I received a supernatural gift. The gift was like a sacred unbreakable bond, a shield of protection, and a love that endures all things. All of the trials and tribulations that I've endured were merely tests that shaped the content of my character and provided me with a unique testimony. With God's grace and love, my story can be used to inspire and uplift future generations.

While I was taking major steps to change my life and live well, I had to go through a process of detoxification of my heart, mind, and spirit which was necessary because my life had become an unsettled mess. I was mentally and emotionally unhealthy. My mind was cluttered, and it danced with the cadence of confusion. I had deliberately broken off key relationships with my family and acquaintances. I had no positive people in my circle. Actually, I realized that I had no circle at all. Isolated away from society, I somehow became the ultimate recluse, physically detached from reality. I spent most of my time thinking about the traumatic, toxic, abusive, and volatile relationships of my past. Ninety percent of my time was wasted on thoughts of acceptance. I felt that members of my family and guys in my previous relationships were not accepting me for my authentic self.

As I challenged myself to blend in as a contributing member of society, my job at the beauty salon became my refuge, my safe hiding place. During each day, as I styled my client's hair, various thoughts of not being good enough congested my mind. The mental hardship of being divorced and having several failed relationships consumed all my energy. Unlimited thoughts of defeat drained the life out of me all while I was being praised for making numerous clients feel great about themselves. I was living in internal conflict daily.

At my salon, my physical body was present, but my mind was not there. The repetitiveness of shampooing and styling hair was something that I could do with my eyes closed. Day in and day out, my hands would dramatically manipulate my favorite styling comb and chrome shears. The ability to transform the outer appearance of my clients came to me quite naturally. While cutting and creating nonconventional hair art, I listened to their requests and tried my best to create a replica of the desired hairstyles. I was skilled at providing quality hair care services, but my main goal was to receive expressions of appreciation that were given at the end of each hair appointment. I liked being appreciated and that's it. I had heard so much negativity in past relationships that I craved to hear a positive affirmation from any human. Words of gratitude were life altering and helped to embed the idea that I had a specific purpose.

My clients would tell me almost everything about their personal lives; husbands, finances, careers, and health issues were not off-limits. I was regarded as a trusted confidant, a keeper of all secrets. Accustomed to candid conversations, I would quietly pray before putting my hands in anyone's hair. I would hope that God would give me the patience and appropriate word choices when it was time for me to respond to the drama that some women carried on their shoulders. I was not a certified counselor, nor did I have any professional training as a therapist, yet my clients placed a huge amount of trust in me. I quietly listened to their concerns with my whole heart. In my mind, it was as if I was spiritually invested in their lives.

Over the years, hundreds of clients had sat in my salon chair. Although there were times that I could not remember each of their names, God gave me the ability to remember each of their stories, which I knew intimately. In my past, I had already lived through the problems that they were individually facing. I could always identify who was the antagonist and who was the protagonist. From the client who was a victim of a cheating husband to the client that engaged in extramarital relationships, they all shared their pain with me, and I listened without any judgment.

I read my bible and my inspirational books regularly; therefore when it was time to give my thoughts about each client's various situations, I would always ask, "Do you want me to continue to just listen, or do you want me to tell you the God-given truth? I can be a real friend and reason with you, or I can just sit here and listen to the trials that you are going through. I'm here for you either way." Ninety-nine percent of the time, the clients would always stare at me with anticipation in their eyes, while waiting to hear the Word of the day. Having God's word wrapped around my heart and ready for battle was truly liberating. As a matter of fact, I would often feel drained after delivering the powerful words.

During each workday, I felt compelled to share God's word, but sometimes I dreaded the response from my clients. It was as if we were having a meeting of the minds, but God's word was more like a foreign language for both of us. My clients would listen as God's word was released through me. At the end of the conversation, tears would flow freely and underneath my breath, I would question, "Where did those words come from?

Wow, God, you are amazing, I'm not sure why or how that exchange of information just happened but I hope it was helpful." When the tears subsided, appreciation and hugs usually followed. There were also those rare times when a client would resist the message and defend or rationalize why she chose to engage in mischievous behaviors or stay with a cheating spouse.

Occasionally, when my clients wanted to participate in intellectual battles about the bible, I would speak my peace, yet towards the end of the exchange, I would retreat back to being a quiet hairstylist. With the client's best interest at heart, I sincerely felt the need to share my perspective, yet I would be sensitive to my client's receptiveness and decide when to simply move on to the next task at hand. I understood that there would always be people who would reject biblical or spiritual principles. Throughout my journey, I too had turned my back on the doctrine of the Lord and spirituality was an afterthought. The righteous path is a narrow one, which has not been easy for me to follow.

Over the years, I have had to spiritually detox and get right with God. My detoxification process included: eliminating negative self-talk, distancing myself from negative people, reciting positive affirmations, exercising, cutting back on unhealthy snacks, volunteering, surrounding myself with positive people, reading tons of self-help books and of course diving back into the Good book.

Notes from the Mistress

ᘓ 2 ᘓ

Chapter 2: His Love

The 2nd Note:

Sydney invited me into her home often, but I can clearly recall one specific time. We were alone. She was in an introspective mood as she began to write in her diary thoughts about her love for Christophe. "There are not enough words available to express this type of love. The love that I desire to explain is like a supernatural force. The heart, mind, body, and soul can only try to allow a glance at something so divine and so pure. This thing called "love" heals wounds from a broken space deep within the core of the heart. This love erased all guilt and shame that once stifled one's ability to forgive. This love moved mountains and allowed rivers to flow.

This love has a unique face. This love has a definitive name. This love has cured the pain that had

*been carried upon shoulders for thousands of years.
Throughout each passing day I thank God, but
unconsciously I question the Higher Power and ask, Why
me God? Why would you love me so dearly? Is this right,
or even appropriate for someone like me to be loved?
Did you choose the right person for this love? Lord, I am
a sinner. I have committed so many sins against you, and
you still love me? Why God? Why is this love so difficult
to believe and accept? I feel out of place being this
happy. I feel so loved that I am afraid to express the joy
within. I've searched this world for love, and you gave
me more than I could ever ask for."*

*It was in that moment that I began to realize that
Sydney and I were in love with the same man. Sydney
continued to write, "When he looks deep into my eyes, I
feel your abundant love and compassion. When he holds
my hand, the bond that I share with you, Lord, is
present. Judgment of me and my past is absent, it does
not exist. My flaws are embraced, and I have never felt
this confident nor have I ever felt this free, free to be
exactly what you've called me to be. Lord, am I
dreaming, this can't be real? Ok, so when will this*

fairytale come to an end?" These subconscious thoughts that continually raced through Sydney's mind gracefully made it to the pages that captured her innermost feelings. Sydney's words quickly reminded me of Burt Bacharach's lyrics to "I Say a Little Prayer" as performed by Aretha Franklin. Sydney had forever on her mind when it came to Christophe and so did I. Here is my perspective of how the love between Sydney, God, and Christophe evolved:

From the moment Christophe and Sydney laid eyes on each other, Sydney knew that one day they would become married and live happily ever after. Christophe was far from perfect, but his caring spirit and his piercing hazel eyes hooked Sydney instantaneously. The deep-set dimples trenched gracefully within his thin brown cheeks were like a daily peace offering. His smile was so honest that if you stared at him for too long the only obvious reaction would be to smile back and wonder why he was radiating joy from within.

Sydney honored the friendship that she and Christophe had built. She deeply appreciated having a nice guy in her life, yet at the thought of taking their relationship to the next level, Sydney would always suppress her true feelings. Instead of engaging in a romantic relationship with Christophe, Sydney enjoyed having a secret crush on him. She truly admired and respected Christophe but was too afraid to ever admit her desires. Occasionally Sydney would probe and ask Christophe questions to discover if he had any special feelings for her. Christophe's response was always something like, "Syd you are the most beautiful woman that I've ever met. I like you a lot, and I'm intrigued by you. I desire to get to know you better. I'm a very patient man and I don't mind delayed gratification. For me, the pursuit is more meaningful than winning the prize. I thoroughly enjoy our banter; it's deeply simulating."

Sydney often fantasized about how Christophe would propose. She wanted to spend the rest of her life with Christophe because he was the most gentle and loving man that she had ever met. Christophe was very strong and handsome, but Sydney was captivated by his intelligence. The way in which he enunciated his words piqued Sydney's curiosity. The tone of his voice and tempo of his dialect was like soothing music to her ears. She wanted to know more about Christophe, so she bombarded him with questions that ignited in-depth dialog.

Christophe was extremely witty, but he was not a chatty man. Without ever intentionally hurting one's feelings, Christophe told the blunt truth. He was a straight shooter even if his words caused some slight discomfort. While engaged in their discussions he always gave a thought-provoking response when it was time to answer Sydney's questions. Christophe's Harvard education presented itself when he would use vocabulary Sydney had never heard before in their heart-to-hearts. She would find herself engulfed in her Webster's dictionary while talking with Christophe because their conversations would demand that she understood the message that he was trying to convey.

During one particular conversation, Christophe spoke about his interpretation of human evolution. He and Sydney exchanged ideas for hours about microorganisms, the Big Bang Theory, and even the creation of Adam and Eve. The biblical story about the first couple was significant enough for Sydney to understand. Although some stories seemed unbelievable, Sydney accepted them as meaningful teachings; they are God's way of leaving a blueprint or guide to help people throughout the journey called life. Sydney relied on the verses found within the Book of Proverbs and Psalms as a foundation to build her relationship with God. Christophe, on the other hand, had studied the entire Bible while attending Catholic school and during his college years at Harvard. He would not argue their differing biblical theories, especially those that could never be proven by scientific data. He loved God and trusted God but he casted the good book off as merely parables, text written centuries ago by clever scribes. At face value, the bible was used to control the masses. It was not to be taken too seriously. It was just a tool or resource for gaining knowledge and wisdom.

Sydney and Christophe held somewhat contrasting philosophies about religion and spirituality. Their ideas also clashed about many different topics. Even with their differences, they both enjoyed listening to each other passionately defend their perceived arguments. Exhausted by their heated exchange, Christophe would always concede. "Ok, Sydney. You win. We can agree to disagree," Christophe would say to dismantle their petty bouts of bickering.

After several years of exclusive attention, dinner dates, and coffee rendezvouses, their innocent companionship had finally evolved into more than a friendship. On the day that Christophe proposed and asked Sydney for her hand in marriage, she waded peacefully in the river bleu as she contemplated her response. The bruising sun glistened on her dark bronze skin as she inhaled crisp air. The breeze flowing through the Haitian mountains gave way to clarity from God. The silence and stillness of the bleu water were as sovereign as the Most High God himself. The creator's presence could be felt as if it knew there was a soul seeking guidance and deliverance. As Sydney stood in the center of the bleu, she boldly placed her trust in God. Grandma Nadeya's words came rushing to mind as she looked towards the sky and waited for a sign, "Wade in the water; there's healing in the water, Sydney. Whenever you are going through something, whether it's good or bad, cast all your worries in the water. God is with you always and if you make mistakes along the way, just remember, He throws all our sins in the Sea of Forgiveness."

Calmly attempting to commune with God, and before making one of the most important decisions of her life, Sydney paused before going to shore to reunite with Christophe. She gracefully stretched her arms towards the heavens, erected her head high and slowly laid her torso back into the bleu as the river embraced her physique and balanced the rest of her body. Sydney's precious temple and soul had reunited with God. She had finally surrendered and returned to the occasion of her youth when she first said yes to God. At that moment, all bondage had been lifted and she was finally liberated. On that day, peace had been bestowed onto every aspect of her life.

While wading in the bleu, a cool sumptuous breeze ruffled past Sydney's body as she quietly reflected on her grandmother's words and completed her prayer, "Lord, I need you now. Please be with me. Give me the guidance and wisdom to do what's right and pleasing to you." Sydney knew deep within her soul that Christophe was the exact man that God had sent for her to love. Christophe was the man of her dreams and he was no imposter. When Christophe stared into Sydney's eyes, it was as if he had already known her childhood wounds and he was aware of the hidden shame stored up from her past mistakes. He somehow knew that Sydney was a delicate jewel. Christophe could feel that Sydney had been hurt and slightly broken. He knew that there was something tragic yet beautiful about his wife to be. He also knew that he wanted to spend the rest of his life caring for Sydney and showering her with endless love. Christophe had never experienced any of the pain, which built a fortress around Sydney, but he was the kind of man determined to tear down those barriers. He knew that only a true hero could cut through those brick walls and reestablish a firm foundation.

Thoughts of the unknown filled Sydney's mind as she exited the bleu. Sydney contemplated her future and drew a mental picture of what marriage would be like as she walked leisurely towards Christophe's stretched out hand. Sydney stood there with a childlike expression on her face as Christophe reached in to embrace and comfort his sweetheart. While safely nestled in his arms, Sydney resisted for as long as she could, then looked at Christophe and said, "Christophe, we're having such a beautiful time here in Haiti. I feel right at home in Cazale. Let's enjoy the rest of our time here and when we return to the states, we can talk more about planning to have a wedding." Christophe stepped back in disappointment but kept his hands placed on Sydney's hips. He was shocked at how assertively Sydney expressed her sentiments that seemed to repress her feelings, so he sought affirmation. "Don't you feel what I feel?" Christophe stared into Sydney's eyes and demanded, "Tell me you don't love me? We've been together as friends for years. You know me better than anyone, Sydney. You get me, and you understand me. Why am I sensing that you may have some reservations about what we share?"

The day of Sydney's dreams had finally arrived. Christophe had proposed. He asked Sydney to be his wife, yet she was too nervous and reluctant to give Christophe an answer. Sydney vulnerably said,

"Christophe, I don't think I'm the marriage type. I'm not good at relationships and you know I have trust issues. Every time I try the whole love thing, I tend to get bruised by love. Are you sure that you want to be with me and only me?" Christophe abruptly responded with deep concern in his voice, "Yeah Sydney, I know you have issues, who doesn't? I'm not like the other guys you've dated; just give me a chance. I won't hurt you." This was Sydney's first time ever witnessing Christophe express feelings of disappointment. Throughout their courtship, he always displayed confidence and never showed inconsistency in his emotions. Sydney's eyes stayed fixated towards the bleu river without giving Christophe her undivided attention. Sydney continued to stare at the bleu while vaguely replying to Christophe, "I want to marry you, but I want us to get married in the states and I want my family to be there. Andi is my sister and best friend and I would not get married without my sister standing by my side. And how can we get married in Haiti, I don't even have an appropriate dress." Sydney thought of every excuse, but Christophe was not buying any of it. His quick rebuttal was, "Why are you so afraid of love? I can see right through you! You've searched for love all your life now it's staring at you and you have cold feet. Sydney, you're afraid. Just admit it!" Sydney did not respond to Christophe's comments although she knew that he was reading her heart and deepest thoughts. Sydney was afraid and terrified of the thing she wanted most, love.

Christophe could see the reservation in Sydney and wanted nothing more than for her to feel comfortable about such an important decision. He reassured her of his love and gently turned the conversation towards the vision of their wedding and future together in the states.

After a long talk, agreeing to their engagement, and deciding to get married in America, they couldn't help but share the news with their family in Haiti. They walked through the village of Cazale sharing feelings and Sydney reflected on her childhood, "I can remember being a little girl and sitting at church in the third row with my grandmother and my brothers. I remember sitting next to Grandma Nadeya, listening and daydreaming as these older women discussed their missionary work in Haiti. I was interested to hear the rich stories about their travels abroad. As they gave moving stories about the mountainous terrain and the inhabitants, all I could do was close my eyes and try to visualize the picturesque descriptions of this foreign land and its beautiful people."

"When I was young, I never imagined that I would ever travel abroad. The thought of traveling to Haiti on a mission trip was nothing more than a fantasy. Now, I'm here with you experiencing what I dreamed about as a child. I can't explain what I'm feeling but the presence of my Grandma Nadeya can be felt. I know her spirit is in heaven standing next to God, but it feels as if she's here in this moment, watching over me."

As Sydney and Christophe returned to their living quarters, the host, Essay, and other family members greeted them. Christophe eagerly shared the engagement news with his family and as tradition would have it, the cultural rituals to acknowledge the joyous moment had begun. Ethnic chants of what sounded like Sweet Micky's *Mache Sou Yo* echoed in the background of what turned out to be the beginning of the first day of

Sydney and Christophe's life together. As Essay and her sisters gracefully prepared a massive feast, the locals from the village joined them for dinner to celebrate the monumental occasion. Sydney and Christophe lived and loved fearlessly unaware of the space or time that barely drifted away. They danced and sang to Haitian Creole folk songs like they were small children from the village of Cazale.

ℒ 3 ℒ

Chapter 3: The Mistress

The 3rd Note:

The Lord's presence was magnified through Sydney's unwavering faith and through her relationship with God, yet she had never witnessed someone who walked with the Lord but put all faith into various compositions of sound. Sydney found solace in hearing whispers from the Lord. The quiet stillness of each day was mandatory for peace to reside within her.

Christophe's knowledge and passion for me brought tranquility into his life. Our relationship was more than a love affair; it was a constant that blinded all sight of anything that was not in perfect harmony. I had been his vice; his harmless addiction and each day he dreamed of getting closer to me. Rocking his knees or tapping ten fingers to my rhythm was his praise to God.

Playing the air guitar, imaginary keyboard, or any wind instrument, expressed that he and all of his phalanges were thankful indeed, for me. God blessed all his days with unlimited tunes. Each day was a new discovery and appreciation for new chords that were realized. He knew me, inside and out.

Christophe took refuge in me. I was his resting place, an escape away from the daily pressures of life. From dust to dawn, the sound of my voice was his hope and inspiration. Before the sound of wakening birds began to whistle, melodies and harmony snatched every moment of possible silence, fueling his mind with sensual vibrations, enough to electrify every minute of each day. To expect him to press pause or adjust my volume was almost a sin. The thought of us not being together for five to ten minutes was like waging war on an opponent who had an army trained in guerilla warfare. The tactics used to feed this hunger for the sound of my voice was incomprehensible.

Yes, that's right, I am his mistress. I'm the type to smile and wave while tempting you to lower your inhibitions. I'm well-traveled and sophisticated. I'm the international type; you know the kind that has range and versatility. Like Betty Wright's song, "The Clean up Woman," I am the dominant force in his life. Some say I can be sweet but also treacherous. The sound of my voice can transcend almost any situation. From sex and cultural identity to patriotism and marginalized economic variances, I have the ability to stir up emotions or unify nations. But in this situation, I am clearly affirming my position as "number one" on Christophe's list of priorities. I am his drug of choice, what he desires most, and there is nothing nor anyone that could ever change that declaration...

     While walking through the village of Cazale and staring into Sydney's eyes, Christophe professed his deep love for the woman that he hoped to marry. In the middle of his heartfelt dialog, he offered an unapologetic confession, "Sydney, I promise that I'll always love you and treat you with kindness and respect. And, I must be honest, I'll only ever have one mistress and that's music." Curious to get a better understanding of Christophe's peculiar statement, Sydney asked, "Tell me more. I'm dying to hear about this mistress." Christophe began to explain, "Well, I know you're aware that I'm a musician and I truly have an appreciation for music. Everything about the composition, the rhythm and all the instruments involved with creating expressions of music, I adore. Music is my passion! When I'm on stage playing the percussion, there's a supernatural force that takes over. When the musicians are playing, it's like a conversation. Each instrument has a distinctive voice or a sound per se. And when each musician's communication is in harmony, it's like magic. When the crowd is up and dancing to the music, they have joined the conversation as well. It's almost euphoric. I must admit, playing music is the best experience in the world and that's what makes me happy. Do you think you can deal with that?" Sydney's eyebrows rose although she was not surprised by Christophe's confession. "You can have your mistress, but I have specific requirements. As long as you continue to date me and treat me like a queen, I'll be your woman; your number one fan."

Immediately after those words flowed freely from Sydney's mouth, she had a flashback to her adolescence. The thoughts of her teenage drama when she dated Jamal rushed to fill her brain. She remembered the strains of dating a rapper and then tousled with the idea that Christophe might also become busy with trying to establish his music career. Sydney feared that Christophe might focus more on the music than on their relationship like Jamal did in the past. Unfortunately, a rap artist had hurt Sydney, so she stereotyped all musicians. Sydney's famous words were, "I'll never date another guy that's in the music industry. They just run through women and I don't want to be with a man that hangs out in nightclubs. I surely don't want to be in a nightclub every weekend. That's not my cup of tea and it's not how I want to spend my time."

Initially, Sydney placed Christophe in a category of men who entertained people by playing music and who get laid because of their rhythmic talents. Later, throughout the duration of their courtship, Christophe managed to prove Sydney wrong. He was all about the music; the music itself was the driving force that captivated Christophe's entire existence. He played music strictly for the joy of playing music. There was no hidden agenda with Christophe, no ulterior motive. It was undeniable that his love and passion for playing music was bound to the core of his existence. The love affair between him and music was more like a stronghold over his life. Music was Christophe's drug of choice; it was his main vice. He craved music like a drug addict yearning for the next high.

Witnessing Christophe's elated demeanor while he exerted all his energy and emotion through any available drum kit was more than a sight to see. Christophe's persona would quickly transform whenever he was given the opportunity to play live music with any of his various bands.

For each gig, whether at a dive bar or an outdoor concert, Christophe would arrive hours before the scheduled time for sound check. He was always the first band member to arrive and the last band member to leave. He explained to Sydney, "I show up on time to set the standard for the other band members, and I also want to be there to help out if any of the members need a hand with setting up their equipment. I have to load and unload a full drum kit. My instrument has many parts. I have to set up the snare, the toms, and the bass drum."

The smile on Christophe's face glowed contagiously as he continued to speak about his passion for music, "I should have chosen a different instrument, but I didn't, so I'm stuck with banging my drums and I love it. I wouldn't have it any other way." Music was Christophe's lifeline and he wasn't afraid to let the whole world know.

Notes from the Mistress

Ω 4 Ω

Chapter 4: Opposites Attract

The 4th Note:

After surviving a stormy season of life, somehow, he walked right into my heart. At the sight of him, I was captured by the innocent stare in his eyes. His dark hazel eyes were mesmerizing like a sparkling trap, and I danced right in. His eyes never stopped smiling, they stayed fixated on me like a predator very aware and certain of its prey. I loved him and I was intrigued by his ability to not stare at my outer covering but rather dive into my body of work from head to toe. He knew all the words to most of my songs, the intricate details of how I am composed and was an expert on my rhythmic anatomy. I wondered, "What is his name, and where is he from?" I prayed to God, "Lord, I hope he's not married." Wives are generally possessive and don't allow me to be my lover's main focus. I wondered, "Could this guy be the man that I've been waiting for? One that will give me his undivided attention. Not only listen to me but also be a student of me. Learn all there is to know about me. Think of me constantly. Want to be around me, dream about me, and obsess about me. Could he be the one for me?"

God must have orchestrated our chance meeting, at church during a watch night service. We all were in the same place at the same time. Sydney was there, hoping to thank God for surviving the year. Christophe was there, praying to start the new year in the presence of God and I was there to exalt praises and worship the Creator.

Sydney and Christophe had extreme personalities and distinctive character traits. They were polar opposites, yet from the first time when the two sat on the pew next to each other on New Year's Eve, the chemistry between them was pleasantly explosive. While peace and harmony were his underlying attributes, faith and productivity were her core strengths. The relationship that they shared was truly authentic. They were so different and exerted qualities that the other lacked; yet when together, their bond was perfectly aligned like yin and yang. The energy between them was magnetic, the force was strong enough to break down boundaries, dispel myths, and reveal hidden truths. I admired what they shared but I too desired love and attention from this good man.

Sydney and Christophe came from two totally different walks of life. Sydney came from a dysfunctional broken home but before drug abuse and domestic violence took its toll on her family, Sydney's parents exposed her to rhythm and blues. Sydney's parents regularly partied and often had "blue lights in the basement" jams, which were the equivalent to social gatherings that always included disco music and dancing. During those events, the strobe lights would glisten while Sydney's father played vinyl records and all the neighbors would squeeze into their basement to fill the hot and sweaty dance floor. The sounds of the Gap Band's *Party Train* and *Burn Rubber On Me* were played on repeat and could be heard from miles away.

No children were allowed in Sydney's basement, yet the scent of piney skunky grass lured them to stand by the basement door. Curious to know what was happening, Sydney and her siblings Ray and Lamont would occasionally creep down the basement stairs to sneak a glimpse of the hypnotic 80s party. They bobbed their heads to the music while pretending to inhale the forbidden fumes. Sydney was fascinated to see the kinky afros and different colored bellbottoms swaying from left to right. At the sight of an adult walking towards the staircase, Sydney and her brothers would rapidly sprint up the old wooden stairs to avoid prosecution from an intoxicated grownup. Since she and her brothers could not join the psychedelic adult disco happening in the basement, they decided to create their own party. Sydney would mimic the dance moves she'd witnessed the adults doing, but her brothers, being a little bit more talented, would breakdance. Spinning on the floor with one knee and pop-locking was Ray's favorite dance move while Lamont would spin around on his head and back for at least five minutes. Lamont's mechanical robot dance moves would always steal the show. Lamont was the best dancer in the family. Andi was too young to dance. She just bounced unsupervised in her play-pin while staring at her siblings exert their Saturday night energy.

Although Sydney had plenty of traumatic experiences in her childhood, she did manage to have some fun. She and her siblings would engage in rap battles and dance contests in the middle of their living room. The competitive spirits within them would emerge and bring out their hidden talents. They did just about anything to have fun in the midst of the drama they witnessed at home between their parents.

Unlike Sydney, Christophe was raised in a stable home that provided structure and support from loving parents. His upbringing included lots of reading or studying, yet music was the focal point of the whole family. During his early childhood years, his parents introduced him to a remarkably diverse collection of music. Christophe's father would spin records from all over the world. Christophe's parents would sing and slow dance to ballads from famous French singers like Edith Piaf and Daniel Balavoine. The Eagles, Crosby

Stills and Nash, Jim Croce, Nana Mouskouri, and tunes from Haitian artists, like Tabou Combo, and Leon Dimanche were played daily. The first record Christophe's father purchased for him, was Paul McCartney's *Tug of War*, which included the single *Ebony and Ivory*.

Christophe's father loved music so much that he purchased various musical instruments and regularly encouraged Christophe and his siblings to perform songs. Fascinated by the popular tunes played on the radio, Christophe's father saved his money to afford music lessons for his children, all except Christophe.

Christophe was the youngest child, so during his brother's private music lessons and band rehearsals, Christophe just watched and waited for any opportunity to mimic what he witnessed his brothers doing. Christophe deeply admired his brothers' band. Although he had no formal training, he memorized all the songs that were rehearsed each day in his basement. Christophe was nervous and insecure about his musical abilities, but when his oldest brother Rafael dropped out of the band, Christophe eagerly stepped in. Christophe played in his brother's band for several years, but he too dropped out of the band when he was accepted into Harvard. Christophe was devastated that he had to leave the band. He was disappointed because he could not commit to the band practices due to starting his freshman year of college.

In an effort to continue playing music, Christophe joined a local band of Harvard students to work on his craft. He quickly learned to play different styles of music with his college band. He and his band, The Cannibals, regularly played reggae, rock, R&B, and jazz at campus events and eventually around Massachusetts. Each weekend, after a grueling full load of classes, Christophe would jump at any opportunity to play.

In some way or another, both Sydney and Christophe's lives were influenced by music. Each Sunday of Sydney's childhood included old negro spirituals and gospel hymns. When she attended church service at Saint Mount Olive Baptist Church there was something about the music that had a profound effect on her life. The music fundamentally stirred the depths of her soul. As the mass choir would sing and exalt shouts of praise, the rhythm pounding powerfully from the bass drum would always grab Sydney's attention. The distinctive beats from the drum drew Sydney into the supernatural realm and commanded Sydney to say yes to God. Something about the music called her to surrender to the sovereign Lord. She willingly said yes to God. She heard His voice through the music, just as she did in the spiritual moment that she felt compelled to give her all to the Heavenly Father. Sydney sang along with the choir and worshiped by singing:

> *Yes, Lord, yes. To your will and to your way.*
> *Yes, Lord, yes. I will trust you and obey.*
> *When the spirit speaks to me,*
> *With my whole heart, I'll agree,*
> *And my answer will be yes. Lord, yes"*

Prior to their engagement, when Sydney and Christophe attended church together, Christophe was always amazed that Sydney knew the lyrics to each song that the choir had sung. He could not understand how Sydney had memorized the words to so many songs for which he was hearing for the first time. Being that Sydney's childhood included mandatory Sunday school and bible study, learning the words to gospel music was par for the course.

With her eyes closed and head held high, Sydney boldly sang, while Christophe nudged her with his elbow "Sydney, how do you know all of these songs"? "Christophe, I learned them, when I was a child. And just like riding a bike, you never forget God's songs." Sydney turned her attention away from Christophe as tears began to roll down from her eyes. Christophe held Sydney's hand and asked, "Is everything ok, you seem to be very emotional. Why are you crying?" Sydney lowered her eyes and tried to wipe tears away as she remembered the days of her youth. Flashbacks from the day of her baptism came to mind, then, finally she answered Christophe's questions. "When I was a child, this music was all I had. When my parents would argue and fight, I would cry out, pray, and ask God to help me. While praying, I would sing the songs that I learned in church and the music was God's way of letting me know that he was listening to my prayers. I don't know how I survived such a traumatic past, but I do realize that God's music was my saving grace." With sincerity in his voice, Christophe responded to Sydney by saying, "This music is powerful, and the musicianship is out of this world. I've never experienced anything like this before. I went to catholic school and attended mass every Sunday, but my church was nothing like this. The music doesn't even come close or compare to what I'm hearing. This music is phenomenal! The choir and the band are tight; it's unbelievable. These are the types of musicians that I wouldn't mind playing music with. They are top tier musicians; it doesn't get any better than this." Sydney agreed. "There's no better music than gospel music. To me, this kind of music is liberating. I feel very emotional while listening to worship music because it reminds me that I should rely more on God. I also tend to reflect on his love. Despite all the sins I've committed, the music makes me feel loved. When the choir is in sync, it's as if they're delivering a personalized message from God."

Sydney turned to Christophe and said, "I have a confession. I believe that my love for God, the creator of heaven and earth, is similar to the way you love music."

Christophe confirmed Sydney's assumption, "I don't know what I would do without music. Listening to music has gotten me through some really difficult times." "Well, for me, God has gotten me through many storms and I'm still standing because of Him," Sydney confidently explained. Christophe replied, "Yeah Sydney, I agree with you. I'm still standing because God was clever enough to create human beings that have the ability to sing and play musical instruments that the rest of the world can enjoy. I think God gave many people a triple dose of lyrical abilities, blessing them with talented voices that evoke so much emotion and tell stories that people can relate to."

ꞷ 5 ꞷ

Chapter 5: A Love Supreme

The 5ᵗʰ Note:

On December 9ᵗʰ, 1964, a few talented young souls entered Van Gelder Studio in Englewood Cliffs, New Jersey. The quartet included a bassist, drummer, pianist, and a saxophonist. With just a few takes, the four men recorded a masterful album that shaped how the world would interpret "Jazz," one of my most endearing personifications. In tune with God and obedient to His call, the musicians gave birth to the legendary sound that has and will forever serve as a spiritual beacon for musicians of the past, present and future. Christophe loves me, especially when I'm Jazz.

Christophe had no shame in expressing his deep love for music. As a matter of fact, every communication opportunity with Christophe somehow turned to music.

The conversation would begin with a topic then he would randomly switch the topic to something concerning music. With each person, whether a seasoned musician or music novice, Christophe would speak passionately about music until there was nothing more to say.

Attempting to educate Sydney about the legends of jazz, Christophe went on to tell Sydney how John Coltrane's album, *A Love Supreme* was, in his estimation, the closest musical expression of God. He explained, "The first time I heard *A Love Supreme*, I must have played that album over a thousand times. The sound of Coltrane's tenor saxophone truly put me in a trance. The musical composition itself was a masterpiece but in the liner notes was Coltrane's prayer to God. The whole album is a very spiritual piece of music."

Christophe continued to explain, "In 1988, while attending undergrad at Harvard, I began to immerse myself in music education. I didn't have a clue of what my major would be, so I enrolled in all the core classes, then on a whim, I signed up for Intro to Jazz. From the first day of college, specifically during the first fifteen minutes of the Intro to Jazz class, my whole world began to revolve around music. The back-to-back events that lead to the evolution of my love affair with music was almost like a chain reaction. My professor encouraged all the students to tune into WBGO, which was ironically the same station that my brothers would listen to. Then, mysteriously, my college friend rented a John Coltrane CD from the library and allowed me to borrow it. I took the CD to my dorm room and played it on repeat for hours. Sydney, I was blown away. It was like a spiritual awakening, a divine moment. I became prayerful and had this sort of spiritual connection. Coltrane's music was composed as if he was writing a letter to God; it was so profound. I couldn't understand the meanings behind Coltrane's song titles: Acknowledgement, Resolution, Pursuance, and Psalm. I just didn't get it. I could feel the music, but I couldn't make the connection. I eventually realized that my thinking was off. And, after listening to the CD hundreds of times, I could hear that the band that played with Coltrane was spiritually arm in arm with him. Sydney, John Coltrane's music changed my life. After hearing that one CD, I knew that I would always pursue music. It's ingrained in me; I'll forever look for songs that move me."

"The following day after my professor suggested that the students listen to WBGO, our college radio station played three consecutive days of John Coltrane which included several interviews about the legendary musical icon. Coltrane died in 1967 and I actually visited his gravesite in 2002," Christophe enthusiastically explained.

Curious to know more and dig a bit deeper Sydney probed, "So would you say John Coltrane's music had a major influence in shaping who you are?" Christophe replied, "No, my parents had the greatest influence on my life, not music. My parents had excellent taste in music. They listened to music that moved them and I am the same way. I can remember my parents dancing in the kitchen while listening to *Bobine* by Les Ambassadeurs." Christophe then suddenly played John Coltrane's album to see if Sydney felt anything from listening to the music. Sydney calmly listened, then expressed her thoughts about the album, "Christophe, to me, I appreciate good music but I'm not really into Jazz.

54

This sounds like sophisticated noise, but I don't mind listening to it, it's entertaining. It's like the musicians are communicating but I don't know what they are saying. I enjoy it, but I like music where there's a singer. I like songs with words, words that have depth and meaning." Christophe heard Sydney's response, but it was obvious that he was lost in a trance and totally engaged listening to the album that he was seemingly trying to share with Sydney. He interrupted Sydney with a thought, "I would love to know what it was like to be in the studio during the recording of this album. It must have been an amazing experience for all the musicians."

$\mathcal{R}$ 6 $\mathcal{R}$

Chapter 6: Le Marriage

The 6th Note:

There is a feeling of liberation and legitimacy when two people enter a covenant with God and consecrate their wedding vows. Intimate moments are shared without guilt or doubt. Freedom to give and receive passion and pleasure are as natural as every breath of life. As she submits to God and agrees to become a unit with her spouse the bond between them creates a source of energy that produces undeniable power. This power is called "love." She becomes like a tree that bares fruit for him to enjoy. Rooted in good soil, she promises to provide nourishment and support until her final day has come. He trusts her and puts his faith in her love. Day in and day out, he works tirelessly while he takes pride in providing for his family. His life is filled with joy and satisfaction because God has entered his home.

This love is a beautiful thing, but I am still there, in the foreground of Christophe's thoughts. I'm not physically present but my voice can be heard. I'm not really keeping tabs, but I introduced Christophe to most of my genres. I expand his mind with my mélange of melodies. In fairness to Sydney, I will give her some credit for sharing many of my gospel songs with him. It's a shame, she has no clue that Christophe prefers traditional gospel found in songs by Mahaila Jackson. Christophe has no interest in contemporary gospel. Sydney has his body, but I have his heart and his mind.

Christophe and Sydney had a private celebration in Haiti to acknowledge their engagement. When they returned to the states, they opted to have a civil ceremony at The Justice of The Peace to legalize their union. Sydney and Christophe didn't want to spend thousands of dollars to entertain guests and profess their love in front of family. Sydney firmly expressed to Christophe, "What's important to me is that I want us to have an amazing marriage. I'd rather us focus on building a solid foundation than going into debt planning an elaborate wedding that we really can't afford." Sydney explained, "I think we should take some of those marriage courses offered at our church. We would probably benefit by having a few tools in our tool kit that could help us during the difficult times that all marriages face." Uninterested in attending counseling, Christophe brushed off Sydney's recommendation and said, "Why do we need counseling, I'm a good man, I don't think counseling is necessary." Appalled by Christophe's confidence, Sydney assured him "Yes, I agree. You are a good man but there is nothing wrong with marriage counseling. Some couples go through counseling sessions before they get married and at some churches, counseling is required before a pastor would agree to perform the ceremony." Christophe jokingly warned Sydney, "Just follow my lead and our marriage will be perfect." Annoyed by Christophe's ridiculous comment Sydney couldn't help but laugh out loud, "Ha, ha! You're really funny!"

Being married to Christophe had its demands and requirements. Although Christophe never asked Sydney for anything other than love and commitment, the unspoken needs included Christophe's consistent desire to pray and have dinner together. Sydney prepared their daily meals and it became a routine that Christophe would bless each meal before they would begin to eat. His favorite prayer was, "Bless us, O Lord, and these, thy gifts, which we are about to receive from Thy bounty: through Christ, our Lord. Amen." While saying the prayer, he would always make the Sign of the Cross over the food with his right hand. After every first taste of his dinner, Christophe's famous words were, "Sydney, this dinner is very flavorful. It's quite delicious! Is there a specific name for this tasty cuisine?" Christophe would then ask dozens of questions about how the meal was prepared and which ingredients were used. He always made Sydney feel as if she was the absolute best chef in the world. Their time together during dinner was strictly for catching up and filling each other in on the events of the day. After Christophe flattered Sydney with his kind words to express his gratitude for the meal that she prepared, he would follow the compliments with, "So, tell me about your day Syd. How was it? What's the latest drama at the salon?" Christophe was so engaged in listening to the gossip about the women in the salon. He would allow Sydney to ramble on for an hour which meant that he could eat his meal, ask for a second serving, and not talk because Sydney had so much to say. Christophe was not a man of many words but when he did speak, he would ask questions for the sake of gaining a solid understanding of the topic at hand.

After Christophe would finish his meal, he always graciously thanked Sydney then retreated to the living room where he would stretch out on his favorite leather sofa, a teal green sectional that he had held on to for at least two decades. Watching Sydney tidy up their home pleased him. As Sydney cleared the kitchen table and began to wash the dishes, he would always grin as if he was satisfied. Christophe tried to offer Sydney a helping hand, but she insisted that he rested. She would not allow him to lift a plate. As Sydney cleaned the kitchen and washed the dishes, Christophe would scroll through his cellphone to find the perfect song to match the moment when Sydney would walk over to him. He had a knack for selecting the right song to create harmony or to create the mood for any given situation.

Christophe's preferred mode of communication was through music. If he had something difficult to say or if he wanted to express his true feelings, he would do so through his music. For example, before proposing to Sydney and during the time of their courtship, Christophe sent various love songs to Sydney, which was his way of hinting to her that he wanted to be in a serious relationship. His musical repertoire was wide enough for him to send Sydney a new song each day to express his love for her. Sydney enjoyed listening to the songs Christophe shared but she had no clue that he was trying to woo her with love songs. She was literally thrilled just to hear authentic new music. After listening to each song strategically chosen by Christophe, he and Sydney would then go through the process of analyzing all the lyrics and discussing each composer's meaning hidden within the words.

Christophe was a master at choosing sentimental songs with deep meanings, but he had never actually said what his feelings were for Sydney. She just assumed that he enjoyed thought-provoking love ballads.

Somewhere along the journey during Sydney's marriage to Christophe, Sydney found herself transitioning from a carefree spirit into a domestic engineer. Married life required Sydney to conform to a routine that included preparing all 3 daily meals. Cooking breakfast, lunch and dinner replayed non-stop, like a broken record. Sydney was becoming restless as the duties of married life were defining her identity. The responsibility of figuring out what to cook and coordinating a meal plan to fit Christophe's diet had consumed a lot of her time and exhausted all her energy.

As Christophe moved up the corporate ladder, from a Business Analyst to a Product Developer of a major software firm, his company gave him the option to work from a C-Suite office or work from home. After thoroughly reviewing both options, and conducting a cost analysis, Christophe decided that working from home offered more benefits. He would save money by not commuting to work and he would have more time to spend with Sydney. In an attempt to please Sydney with his new promotion and new upgrade, which would create an enhanced work-life balance, Christophe gave Sydney his home office then transformed a room in their basement into his permanent office space.

Sydney was happy for her husband; she knew that he was the most deserving person to receive a promotion and perks that enriched the quality of his life. Although the sudden change was warranted, Sydney was unaware of how the change would affect her life.

Christophe was a wonderful husband, but when he started working from home Sydney quickly learned that he was very meticulous about how everything was done. The details were always extremely important to him. Little things that Sydney had never paid any attention to would jump out at Christophe. He wanted everything done a certain way. The explanation behind his unspoken standards was either "efficiency" or a strong case of "obsessive-compulsive disorder." The dishes had to be placed in the dishwasher uniquely. The forks had to be placed upright and all together. The spoons had to be washed with dishwashing detergent before they were placed inside the dishwasher. And of course, the dishwasher had to be completely full or at capacity before the cycle could begin. The bed sheets and pillowcases had to be cleaned two times per week. No shoes could be worn in the house. The ceiling fans had to run all day and the temperature on the thermometer could never go beyond 69 degrees during the summer or winter months. For example, if Sydney was cold during the winter, the only option was to wear thermals under her pajamas. Her level of comfort really didn't matter. Keeping the temperature consistent was Christophe's way of keeping the energy cost down. Sydney often complained about the house being too cold but because Christophe managed all the bills, Sydney conformed to Christophe's household regulations.

Included in Sydney's married life duties were standard practices for cleaning clothes and linens. All laundry had to be started on Saturday morning by 9am and the last load had to completed by noon. To keep the water bill down, it was mandatory to wash and dry clothes during a three-hour block of time. Blue jeans and colored clothes had to be laundered with two cups of detergent and one cup of fabric softener. Towels could never be mixed with daily clothing items and white socks had to be washed with bleach and separate from all other white clothes. Christophe's laundry regulations were demanding like a full-time job.

On Saturday mornings, when Sydney washed their clothes, Christophe would request that his white tee shirts be folded like the shirts displayed on the shelves at the department stores. To accomplish a perfectly folded shirt, the sleeves had to be evenly aligned and folded first, then the shirt had to be folded, but not down the middle. For Sydney, washing clothes felt more like corporal punishment and she dreaded it. To minimize her expected contribution, Sydney would purposely fold clothes the way she had folded them all her life, down the middle vertically, then horizontally. Christophe would eventually refold all of his shirts implying annoyance by how the shirts were folded. Frustrated in the process, he would inform Sydney, "I appreciate you cleaning the laundry, but I'll fold the clothes from now on." Sydney wanted to contribute to the household duties, but all the steps and specific requirements made her feel more like an indentured servant.

Each meal had to include a healthy component, like kale, brussel sprouts, broccoli, asparagus, carrots, zucchini, or squash, which meant Sydney was regularly engrossed in her cookbook trying to learn new recipes. Christophe liked his vegetables and fruits diced thin; he mentioned that his mother had always prepared his meals in such a way that he could properly digest his food. Christophe didn't have a history of digestive or intestinal problems but due to his best friend being diagnosed with stomach cancer, and then dying of the disease, he was very concerned about how each meal was prepared. He enjoyed pasta but rice or potatoes could never be on the menu. Pizza, hamburgers, and French fries were considered deadly and were the cause of cancer. Drinking eight glasses of water each day was the norm and one glass of red wine during dinner was not uncommon.

Each morning, well before sunrise, Sydney would lay in bed and try to sleep through the sound of Christophe's roaring alarm clock. At 5am sharp, the moment he would shut the alarm off, voices of newscasters reporting stories of doom and gloom blasted as Christophe started his daily routine. Without delay, Christophe was up and aware, ready to get the day started.

Sydney would attempt to mute the sound of Christophe performing his daily bathroom routine by placing her head under the covers. This did not help as Pat Methany's *Are You Going With Me* could still be heard playing in background. The first tasks of his day would begin with thirty minutes of personal hygiene maintenance. At 5:30 am, Christophe would engage in an hour's worth of exercise which included running on the treadmill, sixty sit-ups, and fifty pull-ups. Precisely at 6:31 am, Sydney could hear the sound of his panting and walking up the stairs. He then would go to the bathroom and turn the nozzle to the left to get the shower water hot and steamy. After about two minutes, the shower door would close, and Christophe would enjoy the refreshing feeling from his newly installed Kohler body sprays. At 7:00 am, the shower would end, and Christophe would get dressed. By precisely 7:05am, he would plant a kiss on Sydney's forehead, then head down to the basement to begin his work for the day.

While listening to a diverse selection of music, Christophe found value in starting his workday before the other members of his team. As his daily playlist filled the airwaves, he took pride in working almost seventy hours per week instead of forty hours like everyone else at the software firm. By noon, Christophe would leave his man-cave to come upstairs for lunch. For some strange reason, he would bring his portable speaker from the basement with him and continue to play the music while sitting at the dinner table waiting to be served.

Sydney would conveniently prepare a healthy lunch at noon for Christophe. This allowed him to resume work in the basement after briefly eating. He would proceed to work until 7 pm or sometimes 8 pm in the evening. Although dinner would be ready at 5pm, it would be room temperature by the time he would stop working and come upstairs to eat. Christophe's music would still be playing nonstop, as he ate the dinner that Sydney prepared for him hours prior. Unfortunately, this routine went on for several years.

Notes from the Mistress

Ω 7 Ω

Chapter 7: Love Tested

The 7th Note:

I am most beautiful on the day when a bride walks down the aisle. Just before the wedding vows are exchanged, that is when I am fully appreciated. The wedding bliss can be felt as I radiate the airwaves. During those moments, I feel so valuable and so necessary. To see the nervousness of a groom and emotion expressed by the parents and guests; this is the kind of joy that I live for. My main objective is realized when I can cultivate a feeling of longing and everlasting happiness...

All weddings are beautiful. It's a special day, filled with love and joy; however, at one point or another, each marriage, including the ones that appear to be perfect, is faced with some level of difficulty or challenge. Love is tested during critical moments and only the strong or fully equipped will thrive. How we communicate and how we choose to handle each situation will determine whether a marriage will sink and drown or swim and survive.

When the honeymoon stage of marriage had passed and things began to settle, Sydney and Christophe's relationship started to transition from a holiday cruise with smooth sailing to separate ships navigating uncertain choppy waters. Fortunately for Christophe, that is when I stepped in. The perfect opportunity had arrived, and I was there to comfort him during his difficult times with Sydney.

After several years of marriage, things between the two of them had changed and lines of communication were nonexistent. Here's Sydney's version of the crucible moment that changed the course of her marriage:

On a stormy Sunday afternoon, I decided to check-in to gauge the temperature of my marital union. Like a weather forecast, on any given day or any moment, the weather can shift drastically and without notice. The same goes for loving commitments. Sometimes, it can feel as if we are standing in the sunset of the African Serengeti, one lion and one lioness, panting, waiting for the moon to arrive. Although the instinctive sound of roars was felt, constant purring could be heard, signaling to the lioness the unspoken desire. Obedient to the law of nature and respectful to the dominance of his position, she would peacefully follow his lead and submit to the lion.

Then there are other times when the lion and the lioness are in that same Serengeti but there is no sunset, no moonlight, no panting, just a chilling silence. The type of silence that makes you wonder: Is everything ok?

So, I asked my husband, "Christophe, what song reminds you of me?" Christophe's answer and first response was, "Pillow Talk." Ok, so I rephrased the question and asked, "Which song makes you think about our relationship or our time together for the past five years?" Christophe took a while to get his response together. After a long pause, with me just waiting for an answer, I asked again, "Christophe, which song makes you think about our relationship?" Christophe's response was, "I'm still thinking about it."

As I'm staring at Christophe and feeling very perplexed, he begins to take his glasses off, which in code language means, Christophe is going to sleep and does not want to be bothered. Before shutting his eyes, he nonchalantly uttered, "Sydney, let's not have a deep discussion today. I'm really tired. Can't you see I've been working all day?" I was frustrated because Christophe ignored me and had been ignoring me all week. "Christophe doesn't feel like talking or he doesn't want to say the wrong thing, so therefore, he avoids the question completely. I will get no answer this evening! This is very typical. It's the norm," I said sarcastically. As Christophe dozed off, he gently asked, "Is everything ok?" Not in the mood to hold back my tongue, I said, "I'm pissed off because I deserve an answer to my question. If I ask a question concerning music, I'll get an answer but concerning love and our relationship, there's no answer. It's very confusing and it makes me upset."

Fifteen minutes later, aware that I am annoyed, Christophe played a song by Gregory Porter, *Real Good*

Hands, Real Good Man. Instantly, I knew that Christophe was trying to express how he really felt because *Real Good Hands, Real Good Man* was one of the songs that he played to "woo" me when we were dating. It is undeniable; I trusted Christophe, yet I still needed more clarification. So, I asked him, "Of all songs, why did you play the song by Gregory Porter? What does the song mean to you, Christophe?" Christophe stared over at me and answered, "that's the song that I listened to while courting you." Back when we were just friends, Christophe seduced me with all styles of new music. He also had a habit of playing music based on how he felt.

At this point, I was hoping to share my feelings and come to a conclusion about where we stand, "Christophe, I want a change. I'm tired of the same routine every day. When we were friends and going out on dates, prior to getting married, we did things together. Nowadays, you're working long hours, you don't eat dinner with me, and I feel like we don't have a relationship. It's just all work. I want to do something exciting. When we were just friends, we talked about traveling and talked about our goals and dreams. Now, it's just different. All you do is work. I'm very proud of you. You're advancing in your career and you play music every weekend with your band. You seem to be very happy and content with life." Christophe interrupted my rambling speech by asking, "Sydney, what's the problem? I work all day and I pay all the bills! You don't pay for anything but all you do is complain about everything! What do you want me to do? I pay all the bills and you just do whatever you want to do. You have a cushy carefree life, and all you do is complain about what I'm not doing right! What else do you want to complain about concerning me?"

What started off as a calm conversation, turned into the lion roaring and the lioness using all her strength to verbalize the emotions that had been brewing for several weeks. "Christophe, it takes more than just paying bills. A marriage requires the two people involved to spend time together. Every weekend you go and play music with your band. That's not a date! I'm just sitting there, in a nasty smoky nightclub, watching you play music. Even after you finish playing, you are standing there talking with your band members like I'm not even there. You are very happy to play music but what about me? What about us? All you want to do is work and play music. If I mention going out on a date, you just act like you're uninterested or you act like you're too tired to do something fun with me. What happened? What am I doing or not doing to make you not even think about our relationship?" Christophe abruptly interrupted "All you do is complain, all the time. I'm sick of it! You're like the Janet Jackson song *What Have You Done For Me Lately*. I'd rather listen to a dripping faucet than hear the sound of your nagging voice. You just sit around here like you're some damn princess! You don't do anything around the house, except judge me. I don't want to hear what you have to say about what I'm not doing right! I never hear you say I am doing anything right! It's always complaints." As Christophe exploded, I matched his energy. "What do you mean, I don't do anything? I wash the clothes! I cook the food! I clean the house! I cater to the king every day, and you can't even see me, and you don't appreciate my contributions because you're too busy working or playing music or practicing with your band!"

In the heat of the moment, I got up and excused myself from the conversation. Extremely agitated, I stomped up all eighteen wooden stairs and slammed the bedroom door behind me. Christophe retreated downstairs and slammed the basement door behind him. That evening, I slept in our bed alone and I assume that Christophe slept on the sofa in the basement. It was obvious that Christophe and I had hit a low point. The honeymoon stage of our marriage had ended, and we were not equipped to overcome the challenges. I did not feel as though Christophe valued me or even appreciated any of my contributions. I did not know how to express to Christophe that I desired to spend quality time with him.

Avoidance is my natural method for dealing with conflict. Christophe, on the other hand, dealt with conflict slightly different. His way of handling conflict involved withdrawal, introspection, and processing information. Finding an appropriate song would be his first instinct to make things better between us but this situation would not warrant any song. We were not on speaking terms.

The silent treatment was on and in full effect. Christophe and I did not speak to each other for at least three days. There were no words, not even one hi or bye. There was no eye contact, not even minimal acknowledgement of each other's existence. We were just two walls passing by and trying to avoid each other. After the fourth day of complete silence, I began to pack my luggage. I filled two of my largest suitcases with enough clothes and shoes to last for a few weeks. I had decided that Christophe did not care about me, and I felt like we needed space and time to cool off. As I quietly shoved a blue maxi dress, that Christophe had purchased for me, into my suitcase, he entered our bedroom and broke the charade that we had been playing. Startled by what he was witnessing, Christophe stared at me with a confused look on his face and asked, "What are you doing? Are you planning to leave me?" I was still upset by our argument, so I did not respond to his questions. Christophe continued to ask, "Sydney, why are you putting clothes into that suitcase? Are you taking a vacation that I don't know about?" Christophe walked into our closet, took several pairs of slacks off the hangers and began to pack his clothes into my suitcase as well. Hoping to regain my trust and end our state of misunderstanding, Christophe boldly announced, "I'm going wherever you're headed. I wish I had known in advance that we were going on a vacation! So, where are we going? I need to let my team at work know that I'm taking some time off."

As I continued to pack my suitcase, I paused for a moment, stared at Christophe, and assured him, "we're not going on vacation! I'm taking a break from being married. Christophe, you said some very harsh things that I don't appreciate, and I need some time to think about everything." Christophe looked at me with puzzled eyes, "You can't just take a break from being married. We had our first argument! Every marriage has arguments. I'm sorry about what I said. I work very hard and I'm doing everything I can to make you happy. I didn't realize that there were any problems! I thought everything between us was solid! I love you and I want our marriage to last. What do you want me to do to prove to you how much you mean to me?" I looked away and stared towards our bedroom door as not to look at him directly. I said to him with teary eyes, "I don't know if we made the right decision to get married. I liked things better when we were just friends. We did things together. We talked. We made plans together and we had fun. We attended church together. We don't even do that anymore because you're too tired all the time. But, in the event that the band calls you to play a gig, you are elated, full of energy, and ready to go. It's apparent that you're truly happy playing music, but Christophe, you don't even smile at me anymore. You're not pursuing me or sending me love songs. It's like, you did and said everything in the beginning to earn my love and trust. Now, our relationship seems void."

Still frustrated about our previous argument, I calmly explained to my husband, "Christophe, I'm going to spend some time at my sister's house. I already called Andi and she's expecting me this afternoon." As Christophe stood there speechless, I continued to pack my suitcase until nothing else was able to fit. Christophe desperately pulled out his cellphone and called Andi.

When Andi answered the telephone, Christophe kindly greeted her, "Hey sis, change of plans. I've been working hectic hours and I didn't realize that I was neglecting Sydney. She is packing to come to visit you but instead, I'm taking some time off from my job to spend time with my wife and work on our marriage. I apologize for the confusion." Andi adored Christophe, so she agreed with him, "Ok Christophe, I think you're doing the right thing. I know you love my sister and I know you two will work through this, I'm here if you need me. I'll be praying for you and Sydney. Also, Christophe, pray for your marriage and pray for your wife. God does answer prayers!" Christophe sincerely thanked Andi, then ended the call.

Christophe listened to Andi's advice. He kneeled down on both knees, closed his eyes and began to pray. After about five minutes of silence, Christophe looked at me and asked, "Sydney, can I tell you a story about my mother and father?" I nodded my head to show Christophe that I was interested in his hearing his story.

"In 1958, my father and his friends walked through the village of Cazale. While he enjoyed the day with his buddies, he instantly notices a beautiful young girl in the window of her parent's home. My father walks up to the window and begins to pursue the young girl. After several years of courting the young girl, who was my mother, my father asked my mother's father for her hand in marriage. My grandfather gave my father his blessings to marry my mother. Soon after, my parents were married, in Haiti.

In January 1968, my father made plans and prepared to leave his family and everything that he had known in pursuit of the American dream. After confiding in my mother, he left Haiti and migrated to America. My father left my mother and their three children (Rafael, Rohan, and Reginald) behind, yet he promised my mother and siblings that he would send for them.

As promised, in January 1969, my father sent for my mother and my siblings. He sent enough money for my mother to purchase one-way flights for our family. In the middle of the night, my mother and her children secretly packed up and left Haiti. They took a tap-tap to

Toussaint Louverture International Airport in Port au Prince, got on an airplane, and headed to New York LaGuardia Airport. When my family arrived they all nervously went through customs. After all their documentation had been reviewed, they were cleared to enter the country. Their journey to America was a success and they were all overjoyed to be reunited with my father.

Two months after my mother left her village, in March 1969, the Pope visited Haiti. It's been said that, when the Pope arrived, he declared the people of Cazale "his people." After the Pope's visit, the president of Haiti, Duvalier ordered a massacre of the people in the village of Cazale. Some sources say that the government declared that the vendors and merchants in Cazale owed taxes and because they refused to pay the taxes, President Duvalier sent his military to force the people to pay. During this tragic time, hundreds of people were killed and jailed."

Christophe confided in me as he explained, "I'm a product of the love and trust for which my parents had for one another. I was conceived after my mother traveled from Haiti to America and reunited with my father. The bond and commitment that they shared were real." Christophe continued to explain, "My father was an honest man and he was a man of his word. My mother was a godly woman. She loved my father and put all her trust in him. That's the kind of love that I desire to have with you. I found you just like my father found my mother. He cared for her and our family until God took him home. I'll do anything to give you that kind of love; a love that has its foundation rooted in trust. The love I have for you is deeper than words can explain. My love for you is as strong as the bond between God and me. I love you and I will not let you down. Trust me, I won't disappoint God and I won't disappoint you," Christophe sincerely promised.

After I listened to Christophe's story, I decided to accept his apology. I unpacked my suitcases then returned to the initial conversation that we had not finished from three days prior; only this time we had a successful marriage check-in. All questions were answered, and I gained the clarity that I desired to hear from my husband. That evening while resting in the Serengeti, both the lion and the lioness had witnessed and experienced a majestic lunar eclipse. Even if only for a few seconds, the sun and the moon could finally see eye to eye. Both the lion and the lioness dozed off while escaping into an oasis of paradise.

𝒮 8 𝒮

Chapter 8: French Love Affair

The 8ᵗʰ Note:

It was easy to fall in love with Christophe. He was truly a gentleman and a man of his word. So when he promised to give Sydney the world and promised to do anything to bring joy and happiness to her life, he had no clue that she would be the one to show him the world and do anything to bring fulfillment and excitement to his. But, what about me, his secret lover? How would their relationship affect the bond that he and I shared? Was Sydney slowly moving to the first position within his life?

At a distance, I noticed how Sydney's giddy laugh and inviting demeanor were magnetic. She had an innate ability to bring out the best in Christophe. I don't know what it was about her but there was something about her eyes and how she spoke. The way she looked at him and ran her fingers across the prickly grey hairs on his head, while whispering words of encouragement into his ears, was a mystical force. While Sydney made vacation plans, it was me that seduced Christophe to travel across the globe for the sake of love. It's undeniable that I was his driving force. He would do just about anything to nurture our love affair.

To add spice to the marital vows, and plan for life after the nest was empty, Sydney began to think about her future with Christophe. She deeply pondered on the same thoughts, "Where will we retire? What will we do when the kids are away at college? Which country or countries would be great places to settle?"

In her own words, Sydney explains how and why she and Christophe landed in France. Although I was and always will be his motivation, here's Sydney's version of the whole experience:

Christophe encouraged me to do anything that would make me happy, so I pondered and asked myself, "Sydney, what will truly make you happy?" I didn't have an answer, nor did I know how to find the answer to that question. For years, I took independent French language courses and I enjoyed traveling to France, but I didn't have a thing that I truly enjoyed. My only hobbies included watching French cinema with English subtitles and studying French flashcards with the English translation on the back. I used my free time to develop my French vocabulary. I knew tons of French words but actually using the words in complete sentences was quite the challenge. I took language courses through Emory's continuing education division. After completing a six-month crash course, I enrolled in Gwinnett Tech's online French language class. I never got sick of learning French. It was my preferred pastime.

My desires to become proficient in a second language led me to pursue a post bachelorette degree in French. I had traveled to France several times and was fascinated by the history and culture, so I decided to enroll in a French-language program. The only feasible option for studying French would be to take online classes due to my busy work schedule and responsibilities as a wife and mother. The online classes were phenomenal as well as extremely convenient. I learned the basics within the first two years. I learned to read, write and communicate my thoughts in French, but to earn a degree in French, the college required all Literary Arts majors to study abroad. I registered to study in Lyon, France for one semester to comply with my school's rules. When I mentioned my plans to Christophe, he gave me a blank stare and asked, "How in the world are you going to continue to teach at the college, run a business, raise the kids, and study in Lyon? You need to reconsider this idea. I think you are doing too much. You just opened a spa! I'm not sure I understand your plan. Why do you want to do this?" I gazed into Christophe's eyes and placed my hand on his. "This is my dream. I want to live in France or a francophone country someday. The degree that I'm pursuing requires that the students study abroad. Also, in four years all the kids will be out of the house and I plan to live abroad. I want us to live abroad. I have to know the language for my plan to work." Christophe pulled his hand away. "Sydney, you are ridiculous. If you wanted to study in France, why did you open a spa? It does not make any sense. You are all over the place! You need to focus on one thing instead of all these grandiose ideas." I interjected, "I have goals in life Christophe. Yes, I want to be a spa owner and this spa is especially important to me! I am also aware that in a few years, the kids will be out of the house. I absolutely refuse to be stuck here in the United States of America because I never planned to leave. Learning French is a part of my plan. If I could have it my way, I would have many spas and salons all over the world. I desire to own a spa in France, but I need to know how to speak French fluently," I confidently explained. After listening to my big plan, Christophe finally said, "Ok Syd, if studying in France is going to make you happy, fine. I support you. I want you to be happy, but I don't know how this is going to work. Who's going to watch the kids?" I assured Christophe that everything would be ok. "My mother is incredibly supportive of me. She can stay here with the kids. It is only six weeks during the summer. There should not be any issues. You know if I pay Mom, she will be happy to help us with the kids. She will probably encourage us to travel more places abroad while we're at it. We never really travel. We are always at home or work. I'll ask her about it and let's see what she says." With a grunt and we will see attitude, Christophe retreated to the basement, his man cave.

Over the days that followed, I spoke with my French professor about studying in Lyon. Professor Kim, a Chinese native, taught French, Italian, and Spanish. She enthusiastically advised, "Sydney, you would be a great candidate for the French Language Immersion program. Interaction with the natives will broaden your lens as well as enhance your French vocabulary. The experience in Lyon will require daily practice speaking the language. I fully support your decision to study abroad, and please feel free to use me as a reference if needed." After my chat with Professor Kim, I managed to submit all the paperwork to be considered for the six weeklong intensive language program.

The 9th Note:

A trip abroad? Will my muse forget about me during that time? I hated the thought of being separated from Christophe for any length of time. Sydney was moving full speed ahead with her plans. I was there in the background as she wrote the letter for admission into the program.

"Hello, my name is Sydney Ann Marie, a French major post-baccalaureate student. Currently, I'm in my second year of French language education. I'm so excited about studying the French language and culture abroad in France. I'm excited about having the opportunity to apply the language skills that I have learned throughout the past four semesters.

Participation in this international program will allow me to take some of the classes required to graduate. There is a French Culture course and a French Language course that I hope will be transferable to my OSU records as college credits. I hope that I will become fluent in French and learn how to properly pronounce difficult words, and if I'm lucky, I hope to acquire an amazing French accent. My goal is to hear the French language spoken regularly and understand what's being said as well as become proficient in French.

In my current position, as a spa owner and Adjunct Business Professor, my work allows me to communicate with international clients, mentor students and help to develop future business leaders. My goal is to complete the French program and graduate from OSU. I hope that learning a second language will allow me to become more marketable. Developing my French language skills by immersion into French culture could possibly expand my career opportunities. I currently work in the wellness industry and the education industry. I plan to continue to teach. In the near future, my goal is to transition from teaching business to possibly teaching French and a combination of business courses. My real dream is to possibly open a spa abroad, but teaching might be more accessible.

Participation in this international program will allow me to learn a second language with students that have similar goals and aspirations. I hope to have the opportunity to explore different regions within France and live like the locals. Experiencing life in France for an extended period and being able to communicate in French while there has always been a personal dream. I'm hoping that I will learn how to better articulate myself in French.

Thank you for your consideration,

Sydney Ann Marie"

That was a fantastic letter and I knew that it only meant one thing… I had better figure out a way to stay fresh in Christophe's mind. I was confident that he would not forget me, however, I was feeling threatened that this romantic excursion with Sydney might shift where I stand in his heart.

As I waited to learn if I was accepted into the program, I informed my children about what to expect during the summer. The kids were excited about Christophe and me traveling abroad. They actually encouraged us to travel. "Mom, you need a break and we wouldn't mind having a break away from you. All you do is work, study, and yell at us for not doing our chores.

You should travel to France. It is your dream. Mom, just do it. We will be fine. We prefer that Grandma Felicia stay with us instead of you. She allows us to have freedom and you don't. Grandma is more fun," my children said with excitement in their voices. The kids were honest; my life was a routine that included working, cooking dinner, cleaning the house, and studying. Their acceptance of my plan and their words of encouragement gave me a sense of peace about studying abroad.

After waiting for several weeks to finally learn that I had been accepted into the study abroad program, I was fortunate to find two round-trip tickets to Lyon, France for less than fourteen hundred dollars. I searched daily for flight deals online and finally came across a fare that I could not resist. Anything less than eight hundred dollars per person was a steal. When I noticed the discounted fare, I called the airline carrier to confirm the online rate's accuracy. The cost of the flight seemed too good to be true, but when I spoke with the agent, I was given confirmation that the rates were valid. In a state of shock, I quickly ran downstairs to Christophe's man cave and told him about the cost of the flight. He too was shocked and felt as if the airfare was inaccurate. I explained to him, "I'm on the phone with the airline agent. She just confirmed that the fare listed online is correct. She also advised that only two seats were remaining. In disbelief, Christophe logged into the airline's website and after viewing the rate he looked at me, shrugged his shoulders and said, "If the rate is actually this low, which is truly hard to believe, I guess we should go ahead and purchase the tickets now." We ended up purchasing two round trip airline tickets for the price of one. I asked the airline ticketing agent if I could make the reservations over the telephone with her instead of online and she graciously said, "Sure, it's my pleasure to serve you. This flight is full and you are getting the last two available seats. I just need the first and last names of both passengers, and I also need your email address and passport numbers."

A month later, Christophe and I were boarding Delta flight 4327, heading to France. Our direct flight from Atlanta to Charles de Gaulle was full of turbulence. Christophe questioned, "Who's going to water the grass every day? And the trash, do you think I should call your mother and remind her to have one of the kids pull the trash bin to the curb? The house is going to be a train wreck when we return home." I assured Christophe that everything would be ok. "Don't worry about anything. The kids are very responsible. Nothing will happen to the house and our yard will be ok. You're worried about the house instead of thinking about the wonderful time we'll have in France."

Paris

Although we only had a few days in Paris, we decided to make the best of our time while there. We visited Arc de Triomphe, Notre Dame, and visited the famous shops along Champs-Elysees. The first place that we had dinner was at an interesting French restaurant, not far from the Eiffel Tower. When we approached the entrance of the restaurant to determine if we would eat there, a native Frenchman quickly greeted us. The waiter knew we were tourists before we could even ask to be seated. "Bonjour, vous êtes Americains." The waiter must have sensed our American vibes. He pointed to a vacant table, offered us bottled tap water and suggested the special of the day, ratatouille. Immediately after taking our order, he began to mock our English accents. We sat at the table feeling a little uncomfortable as we reluctantly ate an expensive meal that reminded us both of ravioli. I explained to Christophe, "Things are different here in France. Just be nice and smile. We cannot come to France and expect things to be how they are at home. We are not at home. We are in a different country that has a different culture. People have different ideas and different perspectives." Christophe complained, "The waiter is obviously annoyed by us. He's mocking our accents." I consoled Christophe, "Honey, don't worry about the waiter. What do you expect? Americans come to this country and we speak English instead of trying to communicate in the French language. It is kind of disrespectful on our part. We have to at least try to speak French."

After being entertained by the French waiter, Christophe and I agreed that the next stop would be the Louvre. "There's a piece of art that I really want to see. The piece represents Neoclassicism, and it is from the

Artistic Movement in French history," I explained. "Why do you want to go to the Louvre just to see one piece of art?" Christophe questioned. "Well, initially, I was not interested in visiting the Louvre at all because I thought that there was no art that presented a positive representation of Africans in that museum. A few semesters ago, in a French culture class, I learned about how Africans contributed to French culture and society. I also learned about a specific piece of art featuring a woman that appears to be of African descent, that I found to be very intriguing. Some critics believe this piece of art is insignificant but other critics and scholars debate that the art piece represents the abolition of slavery." I continued to explain to Christophe, "The African woman depicted in the art piece is believed to be Ethiopian or Guadeloupian. Her identity is unknown, but the significance of her skin tone and her untold story is rightfully displayed in the Louvre. In my opinion, this image is a reminder of France's ugly past concerning colonialism. I want to see this painting in person because it is beautiful. During slavery, African women were violated in every way imaginable, yet their bodies were desired by the slave masters. According to my research, this image represents freedom and emancipation inspired by the French Revolution."

After visiting the Louvre and marveling at the invigorating painting titled *Negress*, we took the SNCF train from Paris to Lyon. Traveling via train allowed us to experience the beauty of the countryside. The various shades of green pastures, mountains, valleys, and fortresses were a feast for the eyes. We were astonished to see large herds of goats resting together near rolled haystacks. The cows laying under the shade trees and relaxing on the green plains added to the picturesque journey.

Lyon

Our new life on the peninsula, situated at the confluence of the Rhone and Saone rivers, was interesting every day. We discovered the city rather quickly and enjoyed touring around both rivers on our rented bicycles. Each day, we peddled through the ancient roads, sharing the lanes with other environmentally-conscience cyclists, single passenger motorists, and millennials on electric scooters. After sightseeing, visiting numerous restaurants, and touring the different landmarks of Lyon, we agreed that the district of Rhone was our favorite side.

Coincidentally, the day we arrived in Lyon was also Bastille Day, a national French holiday. As we walked from the train station in search of our future living quarters, Christophe quickly noticed various work crews assembling lights and sound, setting up what appeared to be large stages. Out of curiosity, Christophe said, "It looks like those production crews are setting up for an event. Let's go see what's going on. I wonder if there's a concert this evening and if so, which artists will be performing." Inspired by the thought of seeing live French music, we walked towards the closest stage and asked a worker, "Bonjour, vous parle anglaise?" The worker replied, "Non monsieur, désolé, je parle française mais mon ami parle un peu anglaise. Une moment, s'il vous plait." The worker stopped doing his task and brought his friend over to speak with us. The friend introduced himself, "Bonjour, my name is Felipe, what questions may I answer?" Christophe asked, "Is there a concert here today?" As the worker stood by his friend, the worker himself answered, "Oui, aujourd'hui il y a beaucoup de musique." I understood, "yes, today there will be lots of music." Christophe then asked, "Which artists will be playing tonight?" The English-speaking guy pulled out a small-sized postcard from his back pocket and gave it to Christophe. As he told us the time that the music would begin, Christophe smiled and read the lineup of performers. Christophe recognized several of the bands that were scheduled to hit the stage. "The concert is free, c'est gratuit! Be here this evening around six o'clock. All the stages along this road will be full of musicians from all over the world, and after the performance, there will be a fireworks display. It will be a great celebration!" We thanked the two men, shook their hands, and promised that we would return.

Christophe and I strolled casually to check out the upcoming festivities before heading towards our temporary European home. For my summer semester in France, we rented a chic little one-bedroom apartment near the second Arrondissement of Old Lyon. The cozy apartment was located within walking distance of both the Perrache and Cordelier train stations. Our stylish living quarters were nestled on the sixth floor of an ancient building. Somehow, we got lucky and chose an apartment that provided easy access to the university that I would be attending for six weeks.

Once we made it upstairs to the sixth floor, Christophe entered a four-digit number combination onto the keypad of a small blue lockbox, which gave us access into the apartment. We were pleased as we walked inside and looked around the modern loft. We could breathe easy knowing that we were comfortable with the chic accommodations. We unpacked our luggage, showered, changed into casual clothes, then prepared ourselves to experience the national French festivities.

Christophe and I both were excited to experience French culture. As we exited the ancient apartment building, we could hear the sounds and vibrations of Latin music. By the time we returned to the outdoor stage, the streets were more than vibrant and filled with proud French patriots, francophones, and tourists. A lucid energy grew through the crowd as different bands provided grooves that forced everyone to stop in the streets to dance. Christophe and I could not help but to join in. The dynamic rhythm of the music seamlessly lowered our inhibitions. I could not help myself; the music was so funky that I had instantly turned into a Latin dance queen. I confidently let my natural hair down, and joyfully allowed the music to control my body. After one band would finish a set, we would make our way through the crowd to see the next band. As we salsa danced to the tunes of an Afro-Cuban band, Christophe's Haitian roots were on full display. He slowly bobbed his head and grooved with a steady flow from left to right. As he really began to feel the music, he held my hand to swirl me around on the imaginary dance floor. His eyes stayed focused on my mildly erotic dance moves. As my sleeveless light blue sundress gently hugged my thighs, I casually swayed my hips from side to side hoping to seduce my man. The heat from my vibe brought him close to me. Christophe and I were completely soaked, salty sweat drenched each part of our bodies while our dancing had no end. Into the wee hours of the night, we lost track of our conservative

American identities. I must admit, we were truly having the time of our lives. It had been years since the last time Christophe and I danced together.

By the time we noticed our public display of affection was becoming more intense, we decided it would be appropriate to head back home. Our bodies intertwined before we could enter the bedroom of our apartment. No lights were turned on, and there was no need to raise the temperature. The combined heat from our bodies filled the entire space of our cozy summer home. Something about the newness and unique ambience of our foreign abode inspired a profound level of intimacy. Our magical evening and first night in Lyon ended with a passionate, colorful, and loud display of fireworks, the kind of explosion every couple should experience at least once in a lifetime.

Place de Fourvière

After resting up from an evening full of live music and dancing throughout the streets of Lyon, Christophe and I chose to have breakfast at a local cafe the next morning. We sat outside of a small family-owned restaurant, ate fresh croissants, and drank our petit espressos. Our French-style breakfast was authentic and organic, just what we imagined during our talks in the states about what our trip would be like. We decided to visit the church that caught our eyes during the festivities the night before. The church resembled a castle that gleamed from the top of the hill during the Bastille Day celebrations. To get to the church, we had to walk through Place Bellecour, a large square in the center of Lyon, which is the home of two historic statues: a statue of King Louis XIV with his horse, and a statue of the Petit Prince and Antoine de Saint-Exupéry. At the center of Place Bellecour, we stopped at an information booth to determine the best route to get to Basilique Notre-Dame de Fourvière à Lyon. The helpful English-speaking French guide instructed us, "If you desire to see la Basilique Notre-Dame, it is necessary to take the Metro D or the Funicular F2 from Old Lyon, or you have the option to walk up the hill. It's a nice hike, yet not too difficult." The guide continued to explain, "La Basilique Notre-Dame was completed in 1896. You will see, the cathedral is exquisite; it is a beauty. Also, my recommendation is that you take the funicular. The cars have been refurbished, and for lovers, the ride is somewhat romantic." We thanked the French guide, and then began walking in the direction towards the train station. I paid the fare for two one-way tickets, next Christophe and I squeezed onto the first available cable car. The guide was correct; the slow ride up the mountain was very romantic. Couples stood close together and kissed while Christophe and I observed their excessive public displays of affection. After witnessing lots of smooching, we finally arrived at our stop and the journey to la Basilique Notre-Dame began.

As soon as we arrived and saw how beautiful the cathedral was, we marveled at the fact that it was over 400 years old. We then walked up several flights of stairs and entered the architectural masterpiece. What struck me the most were the interior walls of the church; they were all mosaic tile. Christophe and I enjoyed looking at the hollow stained confessional booths, which Christophe told me reminded him of his confirmation ceremony. Me, on the other hand, I had no memories. I just really wanted to experience making a live confession to a Catholic priest. Unfortunately, I could not make my one and only confession; there were no priests present when I peeked through the opening of the spiritual wooden booth.

Christophe was raised Catholic; therefore, he felt a strong connection to God while being in the cathedral. We were delighted to partake in an unguided tour of Place de Fourvière. As we explored the church and admired the interesting piece of history, we noticed there was a lower level of the church. We spotted other tourists lurking downstairs; so, we assumed that it was safe for us to stroll down there as well. The bottom level of the church felt like a global recognition of each country's acknowledgment that the Virgin Mary should be revered. Many renditions and replicas of the Virgin Mary were on display. I wasn't interested in converting over to Catholicism, but I must admit it was beautiful to see the various African and Asian depictions of Jesus's mother.

The whole experience of being present in the cathedral was somewhat angelic. I wanted to take it all in and live truly in the moment. I felt the presence of the sovereign God as people sat in the pews and prayed. I felt comfortable and safe standing in the church and marveling at such a skillfully created structure. Out of respect for the mother of Jesus, Christophe and I both stopped at a designated alter to light individual candles as a peace offering and acknowledgment of the Virgin Mary. Christophe paused, closed his eyes, and prayed silently before placing his candle onto the stationary candleholder. I just watched. I did not say anything or ask any questions. Although we hold different beliefs, I respected our differences. We supported each other even if we did not fully agree with each other's ideas. I had a clear understanding of beliefs and values. In general, people tend to be comfortable with their familiar cultural norms. Some people choose to stick with the beliefs that they were taught during their childhood and some seek to gain their own knowledge and understanding, which may differ from what was learned as a child. As human beings, we typically take on the values that we agree with or that best fit our individual lives. Concerning spirituality, I refuse to be defined by a specific religion. I'm not a religious person, but rather I prefer the term spiritual. I stand firm in my spiritual core beliefs. I accept each person as an individual and I choose to celebrate the diversity of humanity.

We walked up the road to see la Théâtre antique de Lyon after touring both levels of the historic cathedral. The ruins of the ancient coliseum were not vacant. A production crew was testing the sound and preparing for a week full of outdoor concerts. Visiting the Roman theater that was built around 15 B.C., allowed our minds to only imagine what theatrical productions and musical festivities were like during centuries of the past. We took our share of photos then visited two more historic sites: the Lumiere Brother's Museum and the famous Paul Bocuse Market.

Le Musée de la Lumière

We had to take two trains to visit the Lumière brothers' museum, another train from Fourvière, then the metro to the Monplaisir- Lumière station. When we arrived and tried to open the door to the entrance, we learned that the museum was closed. I decided to knock on the door when I noticed a grey-haired woman standing at the check-in desk. The lady noticed me and slowly opened the door, "Désolé, le musée est fermé." Desperately, I asked, "Madame, S'il vous plait, nous avons voyagé des Etats-Unis pour voir ce musée." The woman's eyebrows lifted as she decided to allow us to enter the museum. She calmly said, "Le musée est fermé mais, vous pouvez avoir dix minutes. Tu ne peux rien toucher." I thanked her and replied, "Merci Madame, ten minutes and we won't touch anything."

Our quick visit allowed us to see the Lumière brothers' famous home. The Cinematograph, Edison's kinetoscope, autochrome plates, and other devices the brothers engineered were on display. We had the opportunity to briefly listen to an audio-guide, which gave detailed facts about the Lumière brothers and their inventions. Before the museum agent ended our tour, she instructed us to go to the upstairs area of the exhibition to view some of the very first concepts of human life captured in photographs. The story of the Lumière brothers' curiosity of the world was captured through film and images photographed on various continents. We were deeply moved by seeing a glimpse of diverse cultures represented in the museum.

Paul Bocuse

When we arrived at the fresh market, named after the famous chef, Paul Bocuse, we witnessed several groups of foreign tourists. They were experiencing wine tasting tours, sampling fresh cheese, and learning the history of the local food vendors. The highlighted professionals ranged from meat butchers to specialty macaroon makers like Sebastian Bouillet.

We could not help but to stop and speak with the executive pastry chef after being enticed by the vendor's interpretation of Sebastian Bouillet's artistic display of fine pastries. She informed us that the family-owned enterprise was founded in 1977. The unique offerings included chocolates, cakes, and ice creams which marry creativity with a modern flare. The pastry chef proudly explained that Sebastian Bouillet's specialty is called the Maca 'Lyon, which combines macaroons with salted butter caramel covered in 70% cocoa chocolate and gold leaf. We learned that there are three types of macaroons: sweet, sweet/savory, and iced. This location offered over thirty different flavors, which was unbelievable. We learned that Sebastian Bouillet has nine locations, one of which is in Tokyo at Isetan-Shinjuku. Our curiosity led us to purchase a six-pack of assorted macaroons. I chose the Maca 'Lyon, one chocolate, and one peanut butter macaroon. Christophe chose one strawberry, one caramel, and one pistachio macaroon. We both enjoyed the petit delicacy but agreed the "Maca 'Lyon" was our favorite.

Le Beaujolais

Christophe decided that it was imperative to visit a wine distillery while in France. His exact words were, "Sydney, we can't travel all the way to France and not enjoy wine from the country where it's produced. That would be a sin." So, on one Saturday afternoon, we paid a private tour guide forty-nine euros to join a day trip to the Beaujolais region. After speaking with the French tour guide and successfully negotiating the fare, we stepped inside the coach bus with excitement and anticipation. We were looking forward to reaching our wine country destination.

The journey to the Beaujolais region was long. It took about two hours to reach the area. When we arrived and exited the coach, a husband and wife team, Mr. and Mrs. Laos, greeted us. Mrs. Laos smiled as her husband Mr. Laos welcomed the tourists, discussed the vineyard's history, and explained the agenda for the day. He proudly explained, "My family owns this vineyard, which was established in 1762. My wife and I have been here forever; married almost sixty years and after my parents passed away, we decided to work the land ourselves, full time, and allow visitors to learn about our wine production process. I focus on all aspects of the wine and my wife, Mary, she makes fresh bread and will prepare supper for you."

The wine tasting experience in the Beaujolais region was magnificent. I had never been served various types of wine in a real wine cellar. Learning about le terroir and the wine production process was a once in a lifetime experience. The vineyard owner explained, "The vines must be pruned every year. When you cut one branch you get two new branches and every bud gives a new branch." He continued to explain, "Organically

115

thick grape skin makes good wine. Thicker is better! Grape skin gives the wine its color."

The whole day at the Beaujolais vineyard was epic. I had way too much wine and Christophe must have had at least five glasses of wine. First, there was white wine, Chardonnay, then there was red wine, rosé followed, and finally, we circled back to the red wine. The vineyard owner and his wife explained and demonstrated the proper way to taste wine. We all listened and paid close attention as Mr. Laos gave unbelievably detailed instructions on how to experience wine properly. "There's an art to wine tasting," he said with a stern look on his face. "You first hold the stem of your wine glass in between your middle finger and your ring finger. Then, as you are holding the wine glass, take a deep breath through your nose and slowly inhale the aroma of the wine. As you inhale the wine, you must allow the wine to swirl around in your glass." Mr. Laos paused to observe if we were following along correctly, then he continued teaching us. "After you inhale the aroma of the wine, you must purse your lips together and lightly allow the wine to sift between your lips and rest on your tongue." Christophe and I were so intrigued by our first official wine tasting lecture. "While sipping the wine, try to determine what flavors or spices or notes you're experiencing," Mrs. Laos instructed us.

To really live in the moment, I paused, took an intermission, looked over at Christophe, closed my eyes, pursed my lips, and tried to sip the wine perfectly. Somehow, while trying out the correct way to taste wine, the rosé went down the wrong windpipe and I began to cough and howl uncontrollably. My eyes were watering so bad and I could not breathe – it was so bad that a stranger in our tour group turned to me and asked, "Madame, are you ok?" Unable to respond, I signaled by pointing to Christophe, who was obviously too intoxicated to notice that I could not breathe. Truly in a daze, Christophe looked over at me and questioned, "What's wrong with you? Sydney, I think you may have had too much to drink. No more wine for you. Wino!" When I was finally able to breathe and clear my throat, we just laughed. My only thought of the day was simple, "The French wine is so good that too much of it can kill you."

After walking through the wine vineyard, touring the wine cellar and becoming thoroughly intoxicated, the vineyard owner and his wife taught us how to make bread from the grains and seeds harvested from their fields and using an outdoor wood burning firestone oven. They also served us beef stew, pomme de terre, goat cheese, and petite madeleines. We concluded the vineyard tour by sipping dark roast coffee served in small porcelain cups.

Like a mischievous child, I laughed and giggled the entire time. There was something unique about my experience in the Beaujolais region, or perhaps the French wine had taken its toll on me. As we lingered around the premises, I asked, "Mr. Laos, what makes your wine different than the other wine vineyards here in France?" With a serious look on his face, Mr. Laos was proud to explain, "le terroir, the soil, the air, and the environmental conditions determine the grape's quality. We grow our grapes under ideal conditions, which ensure the distinctive taste of le vin. At my vineyard, Mary and I are honored to say that we do not use pesticides to protect our grapes. Instead, we plant flowers to ward off the insects. Our wine production process is totally organic. Also, the meal that my wife Mary has prepared is organic. Mary planted the potatoes and the carrots. Mary pulled the vegetables from the ground this morning. The beef is rich, and Mary is to thank. She handles the livestock and all food preparation. Mary makes the cheese that comes from our goats. Mary is the one responsible for all of the herbs and spices grown here on our land. This is the only way. It's natural. It's healthy. It's organic."

Although I had tasted lots of wine that afternoon and my cognitive abilities were limited, I was fully aware of the depth of Mary's household responsibilities; but, to gain more clarity, I asked, "So Mrs. Laos, does someone help you with the cows?" Mrs. Laos smiled and blushed as she answered, "I milk les vaches et I must kill les vaches. This is how I feed my husband and the guests of our vineyard." In awe at Mary's bravery to milk a cow or better yet, kill it, I stood there speechless. In the back of my mind, I no longer thought of myself as a domestic engineer. My household duties were nothing in comparison to Mary's.

Annecy

The next day, Christophe and I took a day trip via the BlaBla bus to Annecy, which is south of Geneva near the Swiss Alps. While walking around the canals and observing the waterways, our first stops were the Palais de l'Isle and the Chateau d'Annecy. After we explored the medieval city, we went on a water excursion and enjoyed Lake Annecy with a rented paddleboat. We ate dinner at another lovely restaurant, this time, by the water. We closed our eyes for a few moments and just listened to the beautiful conversations in French. I heard a French couple say, "Nous allons manger du fromage et boire du vin français." What I understood was that they both wanted more wine and cheese. I looked at Christophe and said, "Je voudrais plus du fromage et plus du vin rouge." I was mimicking the couple in my most sophisticated French accent; simply expressing to Christophe that I wanted more cheese and red wine.

While in Annecy, I wanted to go parasailing or skydiving, but Christophe refused to participate in either of the seemingly adventurous activities. "Sydney, I'm not skydiving. I have always been afraid of heights and it is too dangerous. Let's go ride bikes around the island; you know I like sightseeing. We then can have a picnic or locate our next nice restaurant." Christophe was hoping that I would agree with these more sensible options. I kindly replied to his suggestions, "Honey, we always ride bikes. I want to do something fun and exciting. Let's create memories together. We're here in the Swiss Alps. Let's live on the edge!"

Just then, our attention was drawn to a young adolescent salesman who convinced us to rent a petit two-person paddleboat. The panoramic view of the mountains and the ocean made it easy for Christophe and I to agree that enjoying a water excursion together would be fun. It would also be less risky than jumping feet first from a small airplane.

Dark clouds, thunder, and lighting abruptly interrupted our lovely time together. Then, heavy rain showers followed. We were getting pummeled by the pouring rain, so Christophe quickly paddled the boat back to the dock. Our clothes were drenched, and we were completely soaked, but the sudden rain gave us an adventure to remember. We arrived safely back to the dock, grabbed our belongings then ran towards the nearest tree, which provided some relief from the pouring rain. Unfortunately, the sunshine refused to return, and the dark clouds dominated the skies, so Christophe and I walked back to the metro station and ended our adventure in the Swiss Alps.

Eze

Christophe was eager to see the village of Eze that I had raved to him about when describing my last experience in the south of France. A week before my birthday, he reserved a rental car so we could travel to Nice, Cannes and of course, Eze. The drive from Lyon to the south of France was not terrible, although the fees for each and every toll we approached were rather expensive. I spent over one hundred euros traveling to and from our coastal destination. When we arrived at the gorgeous views of the Mediterranean Sea, Christophe and I both agreed that the fees incurred were worth it.

Surprised by the panoramic views from the mountaintop of Chateau de Eze, Christophe shared his true feelings, "Sydney, I never imagined that I would ever have the opportunity to travel through France, I've only read about places like this and daydreamed about what it would be like to visit. It's beautiful here! The medieval chateau is hundreds of years old. I see why you fell in love with this place. France is full of history, and the different towns are all unique with interesting personalities. I like the vibe of each place we have visited. Sydney, my job is remote. I can work from anywhere in the world. I think we could retire here! Which place do you like most, Lyon or the south of France?" I quickly answered, "I like the south of France, Eze, Nice or Cannes. What about you? Which place do you like most?" Christophe gave the question some thought before answering, "It's a bit touristy, but I like it here in Eze. If I had to choose, I would say, I like the area near Old Lyon by our apartment. It's within walking distance of everything, there are plenty of restaurants, and we're near the train station and a grocery store. I really like the courtyard that we visited the other day. Sitting there on the bench under the shaded tree was very peaceful and I enjoyed looking at all the historical buildings." Christophe's words were comforting and warmed my heart. I offered a sweet smile and gently changed the subject when I suggested to Christophe, "Let's explore the local vendors located within the village. We can have lunch at one of the fancy restaurants outside of the chateau, or we can walk along the path to get down to the Mediterranean Sea. What do you want to do first?" Christophe replied, "I want to buy you something nice. Let's check out Parfumerie Galimard. Based on my research, it's a world-famous perfume factory and I saw it when we were driving into the parking lot, directly across the street from the chateau." I agreed with Christophe's suggestion, "Sure, let's check it out. I don't want you to buy me anything, because everything here is expensive. When you convert dollars to euros, we're actually paying 13% more."

When Christophe and I entered the perfumery, we were pleasantly introduced to new and exotic aromas.

We both inhaled the floating notes of rosemary, lavender, eucalyptus, and jasmine as we were greeted by a gorgeous master perfumer. She had a serious look on her face, no makeup on except deep red lipstick. Her hair was slicked back into a tight bun holding her head high. The young woman gracefully exhaled "Bonjour, bienvenue à Galimard! Je m'pelle Monica. Comment puis-je vous aider?" Christophe calmly replied, "Bonjour madame, parlez-vous anglaise?" Before the perfume hostess could answer, I interrupted Christophe and said, "We are in France. Let's practice speaking French. Christophe, parlons en francais!" Then I looked at the French perfumery woman and said, "Pardon, désolé. Madame pouvez-vous nous parler en français s'il vous plait." With a sophisticated look on her face, the perfumery woman smiled, elegantly rolled her eyes, and informed us, "Je suis americaine aussi. You can call me Aleza. Monica is my French name. I'm from North Carolina!" Christophe and I were shocked by how well the American woman spoke French, "Oh my goodness! I thought you were from France. Your accent is amazing! How long did it take for you to learn French?" Aleza answered, "I studied French throughout high school and I took four years of French in college. I always knew I wanted to live in France, so I majored in French Language and Literary Studies. After I graduated from the University of North Carolina, I took an internship position here in Eze and when the internship was over, the director of the perfumery offered me a fulltime position. Fortunately, we have a lot of tourists from all over the world, so the fact that I speak English and French, it was a bonus for landing this gig." I looked at Christophe then looked back at Aleza and said, "This is really interesting. My husband and I are here in France for the summer because I'm studying French at the university in Lyon. We decided to visit the chateau because I love it here!" Aleza commented, "It's easy to fall in love with the south of France. I find the French language to be so romantic! French cuisine is authentic; the spices and herbs are grown locally. The history and culture of France are rich and invigorating to us foreigners. There are no buildings like this in America." Aleza continued to explain, "During my first visit to France, as a teen, I fell in love with the architecture and the cobblestone roads of Eze. Each time I traveled to France, I always visited this village. During my third visit to Eze, I fell head over heels, in lust, with an attractive gentleman, a French doctor. My experience with Brand was magical. He swept me off my feet with his sincerity and gentleness." As Aleza continued to tell her story, I could not help but think about my own experience with a French doctor. Wait, did she just say Brand? I wondered if Aleza and I both had an encounter with the same man. I listened intently as Aleza continued to tell her story, "Each day spent with my French lover intrigued my curiosity. My days and nights spent with him were memories that I will cherish forever. When I returned to the United States, my mission was to find a way to create a life here in France with my suitor."

I was floored by the story I was hearing and extremely curious to know more about Aleza. As she spoke, I began to fall in love with every phrase uttered from her vocabulary for which I was awfully familiar. This was the first time in my life that I had the opportunity to witness a human being that resembled my inner most desires. Aleza was living out my dreams; we had similar interests and predefined goals. To study French and live abroad was the life that I had craved, and to see someone walking in my "dreamlife" was surreal. Meeting Aleza was like a supernatural sign. I felt like our meeting was a confirmation that dreams do come true. God was blatantly showing me that with hard work, perseverance and determination, anything is possible.

As I drooled over Aleza's words, I wanted to hear more about all her experiences while living abroad. I desired to know the meticulous details of her journey to gaining residency in France. Many thoughts raced through my mind. I wondered, yet refused to ask. Was the transition to the French way of life easy or difficult? How long did it take to obtain a visa? Was Aleza in France on a work visa or did she actually obtain a long-stay visa or a permanent residency visa? Also, I really wanted to know about the French man that she had a relationship with, but I decided not to pry. I just listened and felt hopeful that my dream of living abroad could someday become a reality. Aleza was living proof that if I set my goals and keep working at them, I too could enjoy life in my favorite place on earth, the village of Eze.

This encounter with someone whose life and goals mirrored my own was fascinating to absorb. Our paths were similar and our deep love for the south of France was intense. This was the first time in my life that I had met someone whose goals and aspirations were parallel to my own. To see this person living out my dream had truly inspired me. We both were born in America, land of the free, but our minds, hearts, bodies, and souls were very French. Aleza and I were American girls who both had been bitten by the French bug.

After witnessing me melt, Christophe excused himself from our girl talk as we continued our in-depth conversation about France. He walked over to the opulent glass display counter and began sampling different fragrances. Aleza and I conversed about everything from how Charles Frederick Worth started haute couture fashion to French cuisine. We exchanged stories for about an hour, then finally Christophe calmly interrupted our conversation, "Madame Aleza, it was a pleasure meeting you. Sydney, sorry to interrupt your conversation, but let's go have lunch at the chateau. Aren't you hungry? I'm starving." To help with our desire to resolve Christophe's taunting hunger, Aleza offered a suggestion, "For the best cuisine in Eze, there's a very romantic restaurant within walking distance. I highly recommend that you two have lunch there. It's pricey but the cuisine is superb. You will not be disappointed, and if you are lucky, the restaurant typically has live music each day. The same band has performed there for several decades." Christophe perked up at the mention of music, "Live music? What's the name of the restaurant again? Which genre does the band play? Do they play all French music or traditional global music?" Aleza smirked lightly, "The band plays authentic French music and sometimes they take requests. The band has traveled all over the world but, Eze, this is their home and you can see why." At that moment, Christophe had fallen in love with Aleza too. He was also ravished by her sexy words about his favorite topic, music. Knowledge about the restaurant and French band quickly shifted Christophe's thoughts from food to live music. We both were intrigued, inspired and ready to explore. Aleza gave us so much of her time. Her words and recommendations were given like an expert guide, which lead the way for a perfect afternoon in the village of Eze.

Christophe and I followed Aleza's directions and within five minutes, we arrived at *Restaurant Le Mas Provençal*. "Wow, I've never seen anything quite like this before. The ambience of this restaurant is astonishing. It's like a botanical greenhouse. Sydney, I'm amazed at how there are trees and a variety of fresh flowers intertwined throughout the ceiling and walls." Sydney concurred, "I agree. This restaurant is stunning! It looks like a setting or landscape from a fairytale." While admiring the breathtaking canvas, we were delighted to hear live music floating lightly through the air. Our senses were aroused by the sound of classical French melodies. The aroma from the exotic flowers convinced us that we could afford to spend our afternoon sipping tiny glasses of Sauvignon blanc, handpicked and processed from an ancient vineyard in Bordeaux. Dining in such an immaculate dwelling gave us the freedom to indulge in the moment. Hours drifted by as we shared the catch of the day and enjoyed risotto aux cèpes. With class and elegance, the waiters served us graciously, one after another, greeting us and thanking us for spending the afternoon at their restaurant.

Romance was in the air while we enjoyed our time in the village of Eze. Christophe held my hand as we meandered aimlessly throughout the cobblestone pathways around the Chateau. We laughed and shared our dreams of living abroad. The feeling of oneness and the idea of Christophe and I being on the same page brought joy to my heart. On this day, in Eze, I felt like Christophe could finally understand my dreams, and me.

Cannes

After our random rendezvous with Aleza in Eze, Christophe and I cruised along the winding roads of the blue coast in search of the five-star hotel that I had reserved over a month ago. The hotel had great reviews and was easy to find but there was no available parking. We had to park a mile away from the hotel or pay eighty euros per night to leave the car in front of the hotel. The lack of visible parking on the hotel premises baffled

Christophe, "Big fancy hotel, with no parking for the guests and they want us to pay a fortune to park in front of the hotel. I'm confused. This doesn't make any sense," he complained. As Christophe and I walked from the completely packed parking garage and through the vibrant streets of Cannes, all I could think of was how beautiful the Mediterranean would be once we arrived. I asked Christophe, "Do you want to take a night stroll along the strip or just rest after we check into the hotel? If you want, we can wait until the morning to explore this city?" Christophe's response was vague but to the point, "I'm exhausted," he sighed.

When we arrived to check into the prestigious hotel, the bourgeois agent asked for our last name, checked a list of names, and then rudely informed us that the hotel had no vacancies. I immediately dug through my purse to find the paperwork with my reservation confirmation. I boldly showed the hotel agent the receipt of payment for a one-night stay, yet he reiterated the same message, "sorry, there are no vacancies." "What do you mean, there are no vacancies?" I said in a frustrated tone. "I've already purchased a room to stay here for one night and the fees were deducted from my bank account almost a month ago. This must be an error." The agent shrugged his shoulders then suggested, "Madame, you must dispute this issue with the online booking agency that issued this incorrect information." After the agent gave his final words of advice, he made a hand gesture to another couple directing them to come towards the front desk so he could assist them. Annoyed by the agent's rude manors, I demanded in my most professional French accent "Pardon, monsieur, nous besoin de votre aider, s'il vous plait!" The agent ignored me and proceeded to assist the other guests. "Come on Sydney, let's get out of here. We'll patronize a different hotel," Christophe said as he walked to exit the hotel. Disappointed by the lack of customer service, I began to follow Christophe. We both were upset by how we were treated at the so-called luxury hotel.

Knowing that we needed a place to stay for the night, I suggested to Christophe, "I know of another hotel that we could try. It's about a ten-minute walk from here." "Sure Sydney, where to next?" Christophe said with sarcastic enthusiasm. My memory led us two blocks away to Hotel Vendome.

When Christophe and I arrived at the Vendome hotel, a barking Golden Retriever keeping guard at the metal screen door and announcing our approach, greeted us. The owner of the bed and breakfast shooed the dog to stop the uncontrollable howling and opened the front door to welcome her foreign visitors. "Bienvenue!" Before we could introduce ourselves, a huge smile came across the hotel owner's glowing face as she said, "Americans? You must be on holiday." Her vibrant energy and flawless olive skin radiated as she looked at Christophe then stared at me, "Your face is familiar! You have stayed with us before? You're not by chance related to Whitney Houston, are you?" she asked.

I was flattered by the owner's kind words, but I was more so hoping that the hotel would have an available room. I responded to the owner's questions, "Yes, we're American and yes, I've stayed at your hotel before." The owner stared for a while longer. As she continued to look into my eyes she said, "I remember you, you're from California and to live in France is your dream. We met years ago! I never forget a guest of my home! How are you and is this handsome man your husband?" I quickly responded, "Thanks for asking, yes we're fine," then I asked, "Would you happen to have any available rooms for tonight?" The owner's answer shocked Christophe, "all the rooms are sold out. But, if you have time, I will ask my daughter to move her things out of the spare room and into the master living quarters where I live, then you two can be guests in our home." I leaned over towards Christophe and whispered, "What are your thoughts about the hotel owner's offer?" Christophe insisted, "Sydney, it's up to you. I just need to rest, in a bed."

The hotel owner was proud to open her home to us foreigners. She graciously offered, "Can I make you two a cup of café while my daughter gets your room ready?" Happy to receive the hospitality, we thanked her and accepted the offer. "Please have a seat. Would you like le sucre for your café?" she asked while slowly preparing two small cups of coffee. She dropped one small cube of sugar into each of the cups, stirred the café with a small golden spoon, then handed one French style coffee to me and the other to Christophe.

The owner sat across from us and proceeded to ask questions about our future and previous travels around France. She was fascinated to learn that we would be in France for such a long time. She elegantly spoke about her own travels around the world. The joy was quite evident in her voice as she explained how she had traveled to various regions on the African continent. The wild game reserve in Tanzania was one of her favorite places on earth. She boasted on how magnificent it was to see the elephants and lions in their natural environment. Detail after detail, she was able to paint an amazing mental picture of her travels. Our captivation was redirected when her daughter came to the foyer to inform us that le chambre was ready. The homeowner showed Christophe and me to our room. "Up the stairs to the left are the guestrooms that we rent to travelers. Up the stairs to the right is where my husband and I reside with our two daughters. This home has been in our family since the late 1800s. We inherited the home when my father died, about three decades ago," she proudly said as she guided us through the space.

"The first room at the top of the stairs to the right is where you will sleep. Inside le chambre, you will find la salle du bain et le toilet. If you would like to join us for breakfast in the morning, s'il vous plait, please come downstairs between 7 am and 10 am," the owner said, as she tried to remember all of the things she wanted to share with us. Since we arrived, I had been searching my memory for the owner's name but could not remember it for the life of me. "Madam, I apologize but I can't remember your name," I finally said not wanting too much more time to pass before asking. The homeowner smiled and said, "Call me Natalia." "Thank you, Natalia," I said as I reached into my purse for a credit card to pay for the room. Instead of accepting my credit card, Natalia placed her hand on my shoulder, "please make yourselves at home. Le plasir is mine!" Christophe and I thanked Natalia before retreating to the bedroom. Exhausted by the day's events, Christophe walked into the room, removed his shirt and shoes, then stretched out across the king-sized bed. I glanced around the room, and when I noticed the bathroom, I removed all my clothes and stepped into the midsized shower. The feeling of warm water splashing on my body and washing away the stress of the day was very refreshing.

At 7 am in the morning, as Christophe laid peacefully, I quietly got out of bed, slid into my jeans, put on my navy-blue tank top cardigan ensemble, and walked downstairs to the breakfast area. Natalia greeted me before I could grab a plate. The pleasant look on her face was always welcoming. "Please come outside to the terrace, I have already prepared a petit dejeuner for you. Come outside, sit with me," she said with an outstretched arm. I followed Natalia outside to a sitting area aligned with three small white metal tables and two chairs at each table. As I sat down, Natalia sat at the same table in the seat across from me. She curiously asked, "Did you rest well last night because I couldn't sleep at all?" I answered, "yes, I slept well. My husband and I deeply appreciate your kindness." Natalia instructed me to eat. She had prepared croissants and a cheese platter. As I began to eat, she leaned in towards me and whispered, "I remember you very well. You came to my hotel years ago after an argument with a man. If I can recall, it was a French doctor." I nodded my head to agree with what Natalia was saying. She continued to reminisce, "I will never forget that evening when we met. The moment I saw you, I knew there was something special about you; but I must say I was truly concerned about your wellbeing. The night you came to the hotel, when I saw the desperation and pain in your eyes, it reminded me of a time when I had been hurt by love. When I saw your face, I knew you were lost and confused. You were searching for a new life and hoping to start over here in France. I remember your story clearly. You were running from your past and I could see it written all over your face. That evening, I prayed for you. I asked God to be with you and I prayed for you to find love within yourself. Also, I asked God to send you the perfect husband, a man that would treat you with love, kindness, and respect. Years later, here you are, and I must say that prayers come true." Natalia reached over to hug me, and with an assertive tone, she said, "You are a warrior and God is with you. You are blessed beyond measure because of your faith." I was genuinely surprised by Natalia's memories of my past visit to France. All I could say was, "Wow, I can't believe you remembered all of that." Natalia continued to stare deep into my eyes, her final words were, "Your faith brought you here, back to my home. Your faith and trust in God are more powerful than anything that life will bring your way. Your faith is your connection to God. Your faith is your strength, your guiding force. Never lose it and always believe in the Divine."

Universite en Français

The first day at the French university was interesting. On the one hand, I was excited to start classes, but on the other hand, with all the week's adventure, I almost forgot the reason we were here in France. Before I could start taking classes, I had to take two timed placement exams: one was a written exam, the other was a verbal exam. The written exam required that I describe my experience of arriving in Lyon. I had to write about the length of time that I would be in France, my living accommodations, and my first impression of Lyon. The exam was not difficult, but due to jetlag and lack of studying, I had forgotten almost everything that I had learned from the past four semesters. As I tried to express my opinion about Lyon, I could not help but stare at the clock on the wall. The ticking sound as each minute slipped away was more distracting than the foreign students practicing French in the hallway.

After the allotted time for the test ran out, my next task was to complete the verbal exam. The one-on-one communication with the French instructor was cumbersome. She spoke so fast that I could barely catch one word from her entire conversation. The speed at which she spoke came quicker than an auction announcer at vintage estate sale. I tried to introduce myself in French and tell the examiner facts about my life. She could understand the basics of what I was trying to say, but when she followed up with a question, I could only partially understand her. By the time I figured out one or two words flowing from her tongue, she was already asking me a new set of questions. I felt defeated by the end of the exam. All of my progress and practice with speaking French was not apparent during the exam. Anyhow, the examiner placed me exactly where I was supposed to be, in second-year French. She explained to me that I needed to take classes that required me to listen and comprehend the language. She assured me that my language skills were sufficient but my comprehension and listening skills of French were elementary.

Each day included two courses: a French culture course, given in English, and a French language course, given in French. Ninety percent of the students in the French language courses were from various parts of Asia. There was one student from Brazil, one student from Spain, one student from Italy and I was the only African American in my class. If I tried to ask my professor a question in English, she would look at me like I was crazy, then ask "Qu'est-ce que tu en penses? Nous parlons français dans cette classe. S'il vous plait, poser votre question en français!" Basically, she demanded that I ask all questions using the French language.

My six weeks in France were amazing! The French teachers lectured on various topics ranging from the effects of the French and Algerian War to how the French film industry was protected by the government.

Between writing in-depth research papers and taking weekend excursions to rekindle my marriage with Christophe, my time in Lyon was well worth every euro spent on the French experience.

Chapter 8: French Love Affair

ॐ 9 ॐ

Chapter 9: Unsung Hero

A Note About Strategy:

The beauty of the love he had for his people was unmatched. Before he could conquer the enemy or deliver his people from bondage, he had to first win the internal battle, the battle of one's mind. He loved himself enough to self-educate; buried in books, he trained his mind to explore various topics that piqued his interest. He trained his subconscious mind to believe in himself and believe in the good in others. He learned about foreign ideas, laws, and medicinal properties that came quite naturally to him. He filled his mind with knowledge and studied the works of famous philosophers like Epictetus and Aristotle.

He fought and won battles against nations and armies of men who desired to oppress his people. Brown people of color were the people that he lost his life for, but he did not just stand up for people of color, he fought for liberté, égalité, and fraternité for all people.

Amongst his people, people of color, he fellowshipped while strategically planning for freedom and equal rights. He was trusted amongst the authorities but feared by the oppressors, yet the content of his character gained him respect throughout the world.

For the love of humanity, for the love of a higher calling and a higher purpose, we as people must follow this model of love. One which embodies courage, humility, and servant leadership. We must work together and in harmony to make our world a better place, just as he did, as I try to do each and every day through each and every song.

In an effort to understand the man we share, Sydney explains her path of exploring Christophe's Haitian heritage and culture.

Ayiti

Perhaps my interest in Haiti derives from back when I was a small child. Hearing tales of adventures from seasoned missionaries had sparked an interest in the country's untold history. While attending Mount Olive Missionary Baptist Church, it was always fascinating to listen to Grandma Nadeya's church sisters speak with her about their missionary journeys to Haiti. After chatting with her well-traveled spiritual sisters, Grandma Nadeya would explain to me the history of Haiti.

She smiled while telling me, "Haiti, formally known as "Ayiti," which means mountainous land, is a tropical Caribbean island located in North America and shares its border with the Dominican Republic on the island of Hispaniola."

Grandma Nadeya continued to explain, "A long time ago, back in 1804, Haiti won its independence from France, which made it the first post-colonial black republic, a beacon of abolition, of self-determination and of racial equality. To gain its independence, the people in Haiti strategized, fought the colonizers, and defeated the slave masters. In return, France made Haiti pay 150 million gold francs in reparations because the slave owners lost their land and human capital during the revolution." From the look of Grandma Nadeya's face, I could tell she enjoyed telling me this story. She continued to explain, "Instead of industrializing Haiti, building a stable democracy, and investing in education and healthcare, the government spent over 120 years paying off its debt for its independence to France."

"It's a shame that Haiti has experienced such a long history of political instability which includes colonization by the Spanish, colonization by the French, coup d'états, occupation by the United States, dictatorships, authoritarian regimes, corrupt governments, political turmoil, and violence. All of those factors hinder the country from any economic development." Grandma Nadeya continued to explain, "Although the country is referred to as the poorest country in the western hemisphere, I find the history of the country to be quite interesting and very inspirational."

As a child, I was so fascinated to hear my grandmother's teachings. She taught me stories about the bravery and courage of our African ancestors. She explained to me the implications of the slave trade and how Africans sold other Africans as human labor before the Europeans began kidnapping Africans from their native countries. Grandma Nadeya gave me unbiased facts about the motherland and the evolution of slavery. She informed me that Africans were not the only victims of slavery; other races had experienced indentured servitude as well. Grandma Nadeya did not place blame on any country or nationality, she just gave the facts. "Slavery was a means of building the economy. Many nations profited from slavery, and many nations' resources were exploited; human labor was nothing more than another resource. Back then and still today, there are people who have no regard for humanity, but when oppressed people put their faith in God, they can overcome anything. History tends to repeat itself, but we can learn from the challenges and mistakes of the past."

Prior to Christophe and I visiting Haiti, I obsessively researched because I wanted to gain a broader understanding of the country, which seemed to have a negative reputation. Before studying about Haiti, my ignorance caused me to question if some of the negative propaganda was true. I wondered if the country was poor because of governmental corruption, participation in voodoo worship, or if there was something deeper stifling the country's economic development. I wondered if the people believed in God and if so, I wanted to learn more about their faith. As I spent days reading and studying about Haiti's history and culture, I came across an article about the president of the United States expressing derogatory remarks about the people of Haiti. His ideas and words added to the misinformation about the country.

The truth about Haiti is that the country was once the wealthiest colony in the Americas, known as the "Crown Jewel" of France, harvesting sugar, coffee, and timber. Today, Haiti's natural resources include deposits of silver, copper, and gold, calcium carbonate, bauxite, marble, hydropower, and arable land. Its major industries include sugar refining, flour milling, cement, and textile manufacturing; textiles account for 90 percent of all its exports. Haiti's agriculture products include coffee, mangoes, cocoa, sugar cane, rice, corn, sorghum, wood, and vetiver.

Through my extensive research, I learned that the issue with Haiti's agriculture is that the country has unpredictable weather conditions such as severe drought and extreme flooding, which destroy the possibility of economic gains. Today, Haiti is transitioning from a period of natural disasters to rebuilding the country for long-term development. The country is still suffering from the effects of the 2010 earthquake, and most recently, Hurricane Matthew in 2016. Both natural disasters destroyed a significant amount of Haiti's infrastructure.

Inspired to know more and to have a better understanding of Haiti's governance, I explored more research about the country's political system and found the insights of Haiti's current leader, Jovenel Moïse. Media sources report that Jovenel Moïse plans to revive his country's agricultural sector, focus on alternative energy and infrastructure repair. He plans to rebuild Port Au Prince and roll out a national healthcare system. With help from the IMF, the World Bank, international governments, private sector organizations, NGOs and non-profits, Haiti's President hopes to rebuild his country.

One day, while preparing dinner, Christophe walked up behind me and kissed my neck. "What's on your mind tonight, how are you?" he asked as he briefly hugged me around the waist. Taking his question as an opportunity for a real conversation, I just dove right in. "What are your thoughts about the foreign aid given to Haiti? I think the NGOs and the IMF are doing a lot to help the country. Do you agree?" I said as I turned to give him a sample of the food I was preparing. "Umm, that taste's delicious… so, it seems you have Haiti on your mind… Well Sydney, unfortunately, the beneficiaries of the aid are the government officials and a small percentage of the population. The marginalized people in rural villages have no access to clean water and the millions of Haitian people, viewed as peasants, have no access or limited access to medical assistance or education. The government needs to do more," he said as he sat down at the table.

Christophe turned on Leon Thomas's song *Malcolm's Gone* as I prepared baked salmon and a tossed spinach and tomato salad for our meal. We also had a bottle of red wine on the table, which meant we would linger there for a while and talk. We would always have in-depth conversations when we brought a bottle of wine to the table. I sat our plates on the mats across from one another and got comfortable in my chair. "Christophe, I've read numerous articles about Haiti recently, I was saddened to learn about the Haitian children that are being abused and exploited by bad actors disguised as peacekeepers and national workers who are supposed to help them. If this isn't bad already, Haiti also continues to struggle against a cholera epidemic, which some sources say was inadvertently introduced by international peacekeepers." Christophe, learning these shocking details caused me to also search for possible solutions to the problems. "I keep thinking, what could be done to change to trajectory of this country? What steps or processes could be implemented for a positive outcome? Yes, Haiti has been heavy on my mind indeed." I said in dismay but I tried to keep the mood light over dinner.

I had actually conducted several months of research and concluded that Haiti has had a history of being in "conflict traps," meaning too many forces working against their success. Many conflict traps began when the European settlers exploited the Taino Indians and their land. The conflict trap that Haiti is engulfed in existed throughout Duvalier's dictatorship and exists now. Although the country has a history of conflicts, research indicates that a solution to developing Haiti's economy could come from resource revenues from possible oil deposits. Between bites, I asked Christophe, "Do you know anything about the possible oil deposits in Haiti?" Christophe commented, "Syd, I really like this salmon. It's seasoned perfectly. But, to answer your question, actually, the way that Haiti is geographically located has made the country susceptible to multiple natural disasters; yet I suppose that the country could be sitting on an untapped oil reserve. I heard about oil reserves in the Dominican Republic. Both countries share the same island."

As we both finished our last bite, Christophe refreshed our glasses with wine and asked, "So Sydney, based on all of your research, what could Haiti do to change its economic development? I'm interested to hear your thoughts!" He then sat back in his chair and awaited my response. "Although Haiti is a low-income country and resource-scarce, the country is not landlocked. My solution for economic development focuses on export, labor-intensive manufacturing, and services. If the country practiced excellent governance and implemented economic policies, the growth process could begin. If the government provided training to target the needs of high-income economies and made the hiring of its citizens easy, this could be the beginning of international trade relations for Haiti."

I continued to explain to Christophe, "It's unfortunate but sometimes, the international governments instigate and manipulate conflict for their own self-serving interests instead of helping these developing countries that are struggling. The more stable governments should be providing solutions to the problems. In my opinion, the G8 Summit's involvement could help Haiti solve its problems, by creating mandates and policies that can be enforced to help the developing nation. If resources could be allocated towards mining efforts, and oil reserves are realized, I think that the country could escape from economic instability. To improve the country's situation on a national level, the government must work together with the community leaders and the citizens to organize a system that includes vocational training. Currently, there are barter systems in place amongst the Haitians merchants, but I think if there was a formal system that included advanced education and skills training, the economic development could advance at a higher rate."

I took another sip, sat comfortably in my chair and asked Christophe, "you're Haitian, what do you suggest for change to happen?" Christophe fiddled with his fork on the plate to ponder the question then responded, "I recommend that the government provides primary and secondary education, free of cost to all the Haitian youth. Adults should have access to training institutions where they can learn life skills like reading, writing, math, typing, electrical & civil engineering,

157

computer science, medical assisting, waste management, accounting, food preparation, entrepreneurship, data analytics, and sustainability. The government needs to have an incentive to invest in its citizens and provide an incentive for the citizens to pursue educational training as well. To improve the country's situation on an international level, Haiti must commit to stabilizing its government. The international aid and resources must be rightfully allocated to the Haitian citizens. I don't know. That's just my opinion."

"Christophe, all of that sounds very practical and doable. You know how there are non-profit organizations that go to help address social issues in countries like Haiti? Well, I have read several articles about how some of them have been exploiting Haitian children, offering money and medical aid in exchange for inappropriate sexual favors. This is crazy! There must be rules and regulations in place to hold international organizations accountable. Did you know that currently the bad actors have been doing things like this for years? If they are caught, they are only moved to service a different country and not removed from the organization as a whole." I said with a disgusted tone as I got up to clear our plates from the table. Christophe could hear the passion and concern increasing in my voice. He tried to refocus the discussion on solutions. "Sydney, another recommendation for improvement on the international level is for Haiti to build trust with its allies and collaborate with private international resource extraction agencies. Haiti's government should consider investing in the development of mining resources because there are reports of Haiti having untapped deposits of oil. Last year, I read an article, *Oil in Haiti*, where Dr. Georges Michel claims there are many places on the island of Haiti that meet all the geological criteria for the presence of hydrocarbons. Places of supposed oil deposits include The Black Mountains, Les Cayes, the Bay of Cayes, between the Ile a Vache, in the plains of Leogane, and at the foothills of Morne-à-Cabrit, in the province of Grand Anse, the plain of Leogane, the plain of Cul-de-Sac, the Gonaives plain, the Plaine du Nord, Ile de la Gonave, and the Central Plateau of Haiti." Christophe continued to give his advice, "My final recommendation is for Haiti to copy the model of other

Caribbean islands by investing in the tourism sector. Haiti shares the island of Hispaniola with the Dominican Republic whose tourism sector grew by 3.9% in 2017 and has a history of continuous growth. To rebuild the once-wealthy nation of Haiti, collective efforts by the government and power players must be implemented for the country to evoke change."

I liked what I was hearing from Christophe. That's one of the reasons why I fell in love with him. He had the ability to hold intriguing conversations, analyze problems and present practical solutions. I felt my energy refocus towards solutions again and said, "The beginning of change starts with a stable government that invests in job creation, offers free education and access to healthcare. With good governance and policies, a strategic plan and support from the international community, Haiti can begin to stabilize its economy. My ideas may seem farfetched to some but to me change happens when we can imagine and believe in the possibilities."

"Yes Sydney, Cheers to possibilities." Christophe said as he offered his glass up to meet mine. "Cheers indeed," I said as our glasses clanged together for a hi-pitched toast.

Toussaint Louverture

While deeply entrenched in studying Haitian history, I landed upon the name, Toussaint Louverture. I was clueless about who he was. Moreover, I was never taught about his significance in any history class during grade school or during my college years. I learned about the history of Toussaint Louverture last year, a few weeks before traveling to Haiti. Before embarking on an expedition to the foreign land, I absorbed as much research about Haiti as my mind would allow. I watched numerous films and documentaries about Haiti because I wanted to gain a thorough understanding of the country. I was curious about Haiti's political and economic instability. With rumors continuously surfacing about Haiti, I was determined to learn about the country on my own instead of relying on how mainstream media has negatively depicted this country. I surfed the Internet and read various articles about Haiti. I was left speechless upon discovering the history of an African slave named Toussaint Louverture. He was slave-turned-military-leader and hero, who defeated France during the Haitian Revolution. This was groundbreaking information for someone who had never learned much about African history, except for the common narrative of slavery and the stories that Grandma Nadeya had shared.

While chatting with Christophe, I began to share the story of Toussaint Louverture, "Over two-hundred years ago, circa 1791, the Haitian revolution began and by January 1804, Haiti had won its independence under the leadership of General Toussaint Louverture. The Haitian revolution is the only successful slave revolt in history. Toussaint did not just win the war against France, he also made Haiti the first black independent nation, which was a force that helped to abolish slavery. Toussaint's legacy includes freeing people of color from slavery, fighting for liberty, equality, and fraternity. Toussaint is a hero not because he defeated France, defeated the Spanish-half of the island, booted the British off the island, and defeated rival generals for Saint-Domingue. Toussaint is a hero because he fought for universal emancipation and human rights for all."

Intrigued by our discussion, Christophe asked me to tell him more, so I shared what I had learned. "The story of Toussaint Louverture began when his parents were stolen from Africa and sold into slavery. The slave traders bought slaves from various parts of Africa, loaded them onto slave ships, and sailed the seas to a destination where the captives would be forced to work on sugar plantations."

I continued to explain, "The slave ship that Toussaint's father was on landed at the island of Hispaniola, Haiti, Pearl of the Antilles. Shortly thereafter, Toussaint Louverture was born in Haiti. Little is known about his early years but there is plenty of speculation. Born into slavery, Toussaint Louverture was probably conceived in the 1740s; no one knows the exact date due to the scarcity and unavailability of birth records concerning human capital. Toussaint, his sister, and father were sold to Bayon, who was the manager of the Breda plantation, making him Toussaint Breda. It is said that during his youth Toussaint learned how to read, which was uncommon for slaves. His literacy and knowledge about medicinal herbs allowed him to gain respect from his peers and others throughout the land of Haiti. Somehow, through manumission, he gained his freedom in the mid-1770s. A successful coachman on the Breda plantation and a protégé of Bayon, the plantation owner/manager, Toussaint gained power and influence because of his literacy. At one point in time, Toussaint rented a coffee plantation. It has been reported that he was a slave owner who bought and freed slaves, yet at the time of the slave revolt, Toussaint was working on the Breda plantation."

Christophe listened as I continued to share the information that I had learned. "It is believed that Toussaint was a skilled horseman and refined leader. During the historic 1791 Vodou ceremony, it is said that Toussaint could have been present as a silent observer at Bois Caiman. This ceremony inspired the enslaved, who, after this ceremony, commenced to burning the sugar estates in pursuit of the end of slavery. Historians suggest that Toussaint practiced Catholicism and was against the practice of Vodou. Some historians believe that he could have secretly practiced or could have known about the ceremony but there is no mention that he was actually there."

Christophe stared at me as I continued to divulge my findings. "There's little account of Louverture's private life. There are no pictures of Louverture; only drawings and visions of this figure, created by people who had not met him. Toussaint was a Haitian revolutionary that left behind thousands of letters, reports, and documents. History about Toussaint is derived from archived documents, letters written by Toussaint, stories passed down through generations, and speculative stories that allow the reader to imagine what Toussaint's life could have been like during that specific period. Some historians speculate that Toussaint's grandfather, Gaou Guinou, was a powerful West African king, King of Allada, yet other scholars believe Toussaint's grandfather was not a king but instead was probably a prominent official of the Allada kingdom. This would justify how Toussaint and his father could have been aristocrats. Instead of living like royalty, Gaou Guinou's son Hippolyte, Louverture's father was captured, sold, and became a slave in Saint-Dominque."

"Toussaint was a man that established himself, formed great relationships, earned respect from many men, and was given special privileges by his plantation owner. Toussaint knew how to navigate between many social groups since he could communicate in Fon, Haitian Créole, and French. Louverture wanted to have the status of a Frenchman. Therefore, he took on the same ideas of the French elites. He was a peaceful livestock herder and a skilled coachman, yet he would kill in the name of freedom and liberty."

"Haitian museums portray Louverture as a hero. Facts derived from archived data provide insight into the life and legacy of Toussaint Louverture. Throughout the museums, numerous plaques and statues provide dates and detailed information about specific events that happened during the Haitian Revolution. After visiting a few Haitian monuments and researching the legendary figure, Toussaint Louverture, I discovered the history of a hero that I could finally identify with. Toussaint was someone of strength, knowledge, and courage to fight for freedom and equal rights for all people. Acquiring knowledge of this unsung hero was a defining moment of my life. The vision of his greatness, and what he stood for inspired my soul's existence. Toussaint Louverture's legacy is universal and can appeal to people of disparate cultures and backgrounds." Christophe enthusiastically chimed in "Sydney, listening to you speak about Toussaint Louverture and Haiti is riveting. I am proud of you. I didn't know you were so interested in history."

Yes, I was fascinated by the story of Toussaint. Learning of his heroism magnified my vision of Christophe, a hero in his own right. Christophe, like Toussaint, studied daily and was well respected by his family and community. Christophe was a servant leader, a great father, and a staunch role model. In my eyes, Christophe was a modern version of Toussaint. He stood up for justice and equality for all people. Through his music, he brought people together. Playing the drums allowed for creative expression and freedom. The music emancipated Christophe and liberated all who listened.

$\mathcal{S}$ 10 $\mathcal{S}$

Chapter 10: Asia Bound

A Note About Tenacity

Some students excel in academics; their determination allows them to receive honor roll recognition or they finish at the top of their class as valedictorian. Then, there are students who do well in school, but their grades are regarded as average. There are also students like Sydney who struggle with challenges that range from dyslexia to lack of interest in school because the content is terribly boring.

After four years of high school with letters and words jumping around on the pages of her textbooks, Sydney had lost interest in learning. Sydney sailed through each of her classes, pretending to understand the basic subject matter being presented. Afraid to ask questions, she would sit through long lectures and not retain any of the information. By the end of her senior year, somehow, she passed all of her classes with C's and D's and obtained a high school diploma.

Sydney's experience in high school did not discourage her from enrolling in college. Her four years in high school made her aware that she had a learning disability that would force her to work harder if she was to successfully complete college.

Sydney and I have a lot in common. I'm not always easy to understand if you try to read me, but at the sound of my voice, most people know that I mean well. My goal is to connect people and share joy but sometimes people abuse me, take my words out of context, and misinterpret what I'm trying to convey. Here's how Sydney tells her story of perseverance:

After my seventh attempt at attending college and dropping out, I was finally able to persevere and dedicate enough time to complete my bachelor's degree. I chose a major that I felt would keep my attention and be easy enough for me to complete. I was never the honor roll type of student and academics were always a challenge. I have always enjoyed the arts and my right brain was relatively more dominant, so I decided to study Fashion Marketing Management. To change the trajectory of my life, I personally believed that finishing college and obtaining any degree would be better than to have none at all.

Determined to gain a bachelor's degree, I courageously enrolled in the Art Institute. Each semester, I took on a full load; sixteen to eighteen credits was the standard that enabled me to complete the program in less than three years. During my last semester at the Art Institute, the department chair of mathematics encouraged me to continue my education. He warned, "the fashion industry is competitive, I suggest you enroll in the MBA program at Georgia State University. You will have more opportunities once you earn your MBA and if you decide to work for yourself, you'll have a solid foundation to build upon. Sydney, the choices you make today will absolutely affect where you are five years from now. So, think about your future. The master's program is excellent for entrepreneurs like yourself." I chimed in, "Professor, I'm not sure I follow; I'm embarrassed to say this but, when you speak about this MBA, I really don't know what that means or what steps I'm supposed to take to get to the MBA. Is it like the NBA basketball?" The professor's eyebrows lifted as he probed, "Sydney, what made you enroll in college?" I responded, "I'm here in college because I want to change my life. I don't want to struggle anymore, and I think by getting a bachelor's degree, maybe things will change." The professor continued questioning, "Where do you see yourself five years from now?" I shrugged my shoulders as I answered, "I don't really know for sure, but I like business. I've owned two beauty salons in the past, but I had to close them due to the economy and other circumstances." The professor ended our conversation by saying, "Sydney, you're a very bright young lady and I think it would be in your best interest to research Master of Business Administration then study at a school here in Georgia. I have another meeting that I must prepare for. Here is my business card. You can use me as a reference if you decide to apply to any graduate program. I'm here for you if you need help with the application process."

I left the professor's office feeling inspired. Intrigued by his confidence in me, I did exactly as he encouraged me to do. I researched and toured several colleges in Georgia that offered MBA programs before submitting my application to GSU. After about six weeks of waiting, I received an official acceptance letter from Robinson College of Business. Three months after graduating from the Art Institute, I was beginning the next chapter of my life as a grad student.

The first day of class was terribly scary. I felt awkward and out of place as the students introduced themselves stating their titles and prestigious positions. When it was my turn, a heavy dose of anxiety kicked in. I stumbled my words and could barely say my full name without choking up. At that time, my job at a custom closet design company had ended and I had recently taken a position at a big box retailer as a Kitchen and Bathroom Designer. When the MBA program started, I was laid off due to not being able to meet the projected sales quotas. I was the only unemployed student in the master's program. During the introduction I said, "Hello, my name is Sydney Ann Marie, my experience includes entrepreneurship. I've been a salon owner for most of my life and now. I kind of sort of design things, but not really, because they just laid me off. Now, I'm unemployed. Today, I don't have a job and my businesses closed years ago. I've had four. Two shops. Two spas." As the other students stared at me with blank expressions on their faces, I felt so stupid just rambling out words, but I really wanted to be there. I wanted to learn and I wanted to challenge myself. No one in my immediate family had attended graduate school to study business, so I was up for the experience. My only issue was doubt. I wondered if I could really finish the program. Each day I questioned myself, "I don't know if I can do this. I have never heard of "time value of money." How in the world can I balance out something that I can't even understand? Income statements and owner's equity... what are you supposed to do with that?"

After my epic introduction, the professor explained that our class would be broken into groups of five or six. He warned, "Look at the people around you. Everyone sitting in this class today, they're all a part of your team. You cannot complete this program alone; there's too much work for one person. You will work together as a team. The team you start with is the team that you'll graduate with. There are forty students in this class, not all of you will graduate. For some, the work will be too difficult, and you'll quit. For others, your jobs will become more demanding as you progress through this program, and you'll have to make a difficult decision on whether to stay or drop out. Every year, and I've been teaching here for twenty years now, there's someone that dies, has a baby or gets a divorce. It's inevitable; it happens every year." The professor continued to instruct, "Be kind to one another. You all come from different walks of life, different experiences and different ways of problem solving. The goal is to learn from one another."

After the professor gave his speech about leadership, it was time for each team to meet and come up with a team name. I was placed on a team with an older guy from Munich, Germany, a beautiful young lady from Afghanistan, a French-speaking guy from Senegal, a guy from Brooklyn, New York and a guy from North Carolina. To help with choosing a name, we had to find something that we all had in common. There was nothing that our team could agree upon other than the idea that we all liked beer. Therefore, we agreed that our team name would be Team Bier. When we introduced ourselves as a group to the rest of our cohort, they all were amused by our team name. And yes, we did drink plenty of beer throughout our seventeen months together.

The rigorous MBA program pushed me beyond my limits. There were plenty of late nights at the college, with my team, trying our best to solve complex problems. We regularly met with other teams to review case studies and compare balance sheets and income statements. I personally had many nights where the stress of college brought me to tears. Christophe would encourage me to keep pressing forward. At those moments, when I contemplated calling it quits, he would step in and explain accounting concepts and formulas for which he had learned decades ago at Harvard. Without Christophe's help, I can't say that I would have completed the master's program. He was dedicated to ensuring that I succeeded. Therefore, he took pride in helping me to grasp difficult concepts. He also managed all the household chores like cooking dinner and handling the laundry, so I could focus on my studies.

Finally, after seventeen months and hundreds of case studies, our cohort was preparing for the final phase of the master's program. We were a week away from our international residency, which would take place in Asia. The goal of the residency abroad was to broaden our horizons and see how companies abroad do business. Our itinerary included three days in Vietnam, four days in Cambodia and four days in Thailand. Initially, I was not excited about traveling to Asia. Perhaps, I was nervous about the journey because I didn't know much history of any of the countries and there would be a language barrier that would limit any possible interaction. After telling Christophe how I felt about traveling to Asia, he reminded me, "Your sister, Andi, is in Shanghai. You should try to visit her. You'll be on the same continent; you should make plans to spend time with her." That was something that I had not thought of. It would be nice to see my sister, however, my rational self started to move to the forefront. "I don't know if I should go to Asia, I think it will cost too much and I'm unemployed. We can't afford it, can we?" Christophe looked over at me and said, "We have some extra money in our savings account. If you want to see your sister first before meeting your cohort, I'll book your flight for you." My heart fluttered with joy. Not only was I going to see my sister soon, my husband was in full support and actually helping to make it happen.

Christophe surfed the internet until he could find a reasonably priced flight from Atlanta to Shanghai and when he located an inexpensive airfare, he purchased it. I asked Christophe, "Do we have enough money in the bank for both of us to fly to Asia? It would be nice if we could go together." He replied, "Sydney, you need to go to Asia, it's a requirement for your degree. Spending quality time with your sister is a gift from me. You've worked so hard to get this far. Go and enjoy yourself, it will be more than worth it. You haven't seen Andi since your last girls' trip to Europe." And that's exactly what I did.

Shanghai, China

As a gift from Christophe, he and Andi handled all the travel arrangements for me to participate in the international residency. The plan was for me to fly into China to spend time with Andi for a few days. Next, I would travel to Vietnam to meet my classmates; then, our entire cohort would travel as a group to Cambodia and Thailand.

Thanks to my well-traveled sister and husband, I landed across the globe, in Asia, after about eighteen hours of flying economy class on a budget airline carrier. I didn't mind the tight seats, the turbulence, or the layover in Tokyo. My main concern was locating Andi when I arrived at the airport in Shanghai. My fear of getting lost and sitting in the airport for hours was manifested as the Chinese customs officers detained me because my departing flight and airport, leaving from China, was different than my arrival airport. The way my flights and itinerary had been planned was illegal and I was breaking Chinese law. Apparently, foreigners can't enter and exit the country through different airports; this was strictly prohibited.

For the first time in my life, I felt completely incompetent. I was unable to speak Mandarin and therefore unable to communicate with the airport officials. From my perspective, I was at a disadvantage; I couldn't express my desperation to connect with my sister who was moderately fluent in Chinese. All I could do was just stand there, speechless as the agents aggressively yelled Mandarin phrases at me. I was frustrated by my inability to understand anything that they were saying but my intuition guided me to give one of the agents a small piece of paper with Andi's telephone number scribbled across it, in blue ink. While stuck, not being able to pass through customs, and experiencing mass miscommunication, I gestured with my pinky at my mouth and thumb near my ear, to signal if I could make a phone call. After glancing at the number, pausing for about three minutes, then walking a few feet away and returning to where I was sitting, the Chinese agent pulled out his cellphone to call Andi.

Thankfully, Andi answered on the first ring. The Chinese agent proceeded to speak with Andi and after about fifteen minutes of toiling back and forth, Andi must have asked the agent if she could speak with me. The agent handed me his small black flip phone and then I heard Andi's voice. Thoughts of not being able to see her and possibly going to jail caused my adrenaline to speed up. I worried about what was next. Andi quickly explained, "Sydney, stay calm, don't say anything. Just listen to me. To get you through customs, basically the Chinese agent is demanding money. He's asking for one hundred USD or seven hundred renminbi. I have RMB, but he won't let you meet me to give him the money. If you don't have the cash on you, you'll have to go to an ATM and withdraw money or the agent won't allow you access into China. He's saying you'll have to purchase a new flight and go back to America or pay him. He's going to walk with you to the nearest ATM. Just do what I'm telling you to do. Don't worry, I'm here at the airport and I'll be waiting for you at the baggage claim area."

I have always trusted Andi with everything. She has been my hero and my inspiration for as long as I can remember, but I must admit, I was very disappointed about the extortion scheme that I was experiencing. I didn't have any money in the bank, nor did I have a job. I worried that if I called Christophe, he would have a heart attack if I asked him to transfer money into my account, so I could pay the Chinese agent to get through customs. Instead of going through the hassle of calling and explaining all the details to Christophe, I reached into the front pocket of my black fanny pack to give the Chinese agent what would have been my spending money during the international residency. Stored between the pages of my passport, all I had was a one-hundred-dollar bill that I reluctantly handed over to the indecent agent. The moment his hands touched the money, his stern facial expression shifted to a crooked smile as he spoke with a wispy Chinese accent saying to me, "Thank you for the money, in God we trust."

Without a fight or even standing up for my rights, I allowed the agent to rob me, leaving me with nothing more than a jaded perspective about China before I could truly experience the country.

I finally united with Andi and the joy of our sisterhood bond overshadowed the corrupt behavior of the Chinese agent. We hugged and she encouraged me,

"Syd, don't worry about the money. You won't need any while here with me and I'll give you back whatever you paid to that agent. Please don't let that incident ruin your vacation. I have planned so much for us to do."

I was both exhausted and jetlagged when we arrived at Andi's posh two-story apartment. Upon opening the door, I could hear light Asian music playing in the background. There were floor to ceiling windows at the kitchen creating an atrium effect. The architectural design of Andi's home was very modern and feng shui, but the structural framework exuded ancient Chinese engineering. I could see that Andi took the time to create a sense of Zen in her home. I explained to Andi, "Sis, I just want to rest. We don't have to do any sightseeing. I'm just happy to be here in China with you! We have not seen each other in almost ten years. The last time we were together was during our second girls' trip to Europe." Andi agreed, "Ok Syd, we don't have to go see the main tourist attractions, but I know how much you love spas. Let's at least go visit a nice one. There's a high-end hotel that serves the best cold and warm teas in their spa. The spa is super cute, and I really want you to experience it. We do not have to get spa services, but we can act like hotel guests to utilize the spa facility. Trust me, it's amazing. I promise, you'll be blown away."

The next day, we staggered out of Andi's apartment after eating a light breakfast. Andi was a vegetarian. Green tea and a variety of fruit was the first meal of the day. We stood in the street to flag down a yellow cab to transport us to St. Regis. Everything about the hotel and spa was magnificent. The Asian inspired décor and ambiance were like something from a Hollywood movie.

Hoping not to get stopped by one of the hotel agents or the hotel manager, Andi and I casually took the elevator to the floor named "Wellness." We were immediately hypnotized by the sound of soothing flutes and the aroma of fresh orchards flowing through the air. Two young Asian women were at the doors gracefully bowing their heads to greet us. They were dressed in sophisticated matching black kimonos and ornate embroidered satin slippers. Their customer service skills were phenomenal. After they gave us a private tour of the spa, we sat in the art deco lounge area and sipped various types of tea for hours. By the time they had served us every flavor available, we had become connoisseurs of the unique delicacy. I had never tasted so many variations of brewed herbs; it was an experience that changed my outlook on tea consumption.

After we binged on custom Chinese teas, we decided to eat at the hotel's restaurant. Andi ordered Lo Mein for us then began to probe "So, how's married life? What's going on with you and my brother-in-law? I wish Christophe could have joined you on the trip." I paused, took a deep breath "Andi, I needed this time for myself. I adore Christophe, I think we have a loving relationship. I've come to terms with the fact that music is his mistress, however, sometimes I wish I could move him the way she does. Honestly, it's more like Christophe is married to music and I am the woman on the side." Andi had a concerned look on her face as she sought clarification, "What exactly do you mean Sydney?" I explained, "In our marriage, the music plays constantly to the point where I can't hear my own thoughts. Sometimes it feels like I'm competing with music for Christophe's time and attention." "If that's your biggest problem or issue, it sounds like you and Christophe are doing just fine." Andi rolled her eyes and laughed at my venting.

Each moment of our time together in Shanghai was either full of reminiscing about our childhood, exploring new places, or creating new memories. Although Andi is my younger sister, she had truly become my best friend.

The final day with my sister was bittersweet. Our days of exploring the Chinese markets and late nights of laughing were slowly coming to an end. I didn't want to leave my sister's company. Seeing her first, before I traveled through Asia, gave me confidence about the remainder of my time on the continent that she called her second home. Andi had lived one year in Japan, one year in Korea, one year in Thailand, and at least eight years in China working as an English teacher. She had traveled all over the world, so before I departed, she instructed me on how to navigate my way to Vietnam. "First we'll have to convert some money. We should do this before you get to Siem Reap. Everything there is super inexpensive, so you won't need much money. While we're at it, we may as well convert money for the other countries that you'll visit. In my opinion, it's best not to use American dollars because the natives might try to take advantage of you."

Andi handled everything, including communicating with the currency agent, paying the conversion fees, and lining my purse with currency for three different countries. My sister knew that I was green concerning travel in Asia. She gave me a list of instructions and key phrases to help with asking for directions and saying common terms that were the equivalent to saying please and thank you.

As the time for my departure had arrived, my sister and I teared up as we prepared to travel in separate directions. We both could not hold back our emotions. Andi was so happy to have a familiar face to hang out with but sad that our sister-time together was ending. Me, on the other hand, I cried tears of joy because I was so proud of the woman that Andi had become. I admired her bravery to live and teach abroad. Her ability to adapt to several different Asian cultures and learn three different languages was quite impressive. Spending time with Andi and seeing how well she had adjusted to life as an expat had a profound impact on my perspective about what is possible and what one can achieve. My love and respect for my sister evolved. Witnessing her courage had changed my life forever.

Vietnam Experience

The direct flight from Shanghai into Vietnam was peaceful and I had no issues with customs. As I walked through the terminal, I located the first available private driver, gave him the address to the Intercontinental Hotel and followed him to his parked taxi. We drove about forty minutes through Siem Reap to arrive at the hotel where I would be meeting my classmates. I called Christophe to tell him that I had arrived safely, but he did not answer.

My time spent in Vietnam was extremely eye opening. The international residency was kicked off by two planned excursions. The first was a tour of the Mekong Delta and the second was a visit to the historic Cu Chi Tunnels. After we traveled to the historic landmark where the Vietnamese soldiers defeated the

American troops, during the Vietnam War, we ate lunch at a quaint little restaurant, the Saigon River. The authentic food was delicious.

As we traveled to our next destination, the tour bus veered off the path into a hidden rural village. We stopped at a local shop where several skilled workers were creating art sculptures made with baked eggshells and rice grains. It was interesting to see the artists create such detailed work.

Witnessing the assembly line in the rural village gave me inspiration for my future trip to Haiti. I was amazed at how the natives in the village used natural resources to support their economic development. In America, we would consider eggshells trash and the only purpose for rice would be for consumption.

We stood outside and observed the art production process before entering the makeshift souvenir shop. The unique assembly line consisted of one person who was responsible for drying and cracking the eggshells, one person who sat and sketched the design, one person who strategically placed the dried eggshells on a plank-like surface, and one person who slowly brushed various hues of acrylic paint onto the eggshells. The last two people on the assembly line were a guy who prepared the planks and another guy who polished the final products with a clear lacquer. I watched in admiration, as the workers paid no attention to me staring intently, while their eyes stayed focused on every detail of their specific job duties.

Intrigued by the workers' dedication to detail, I decided to patronize the local art vendor. I kindly offered the merchant about fifty thousand Vietnamese dongs for a small art structure that could fit securely into my purse. He gladly accepted my offer and began to wrap the art with two thin white sheets of wrapping paper. After receiving the receipt for my purchase, I got back on the tour bus and waited patiently until it was time to depart and head to the next destination.

The boat ride through the Mekong Delta was fascinating. The guide explained the history before taking us through a coconut plantation where we experienced another rural production process. The natives were proud to teach us about all the many uses of coconuts. I had never witnessed sustainable farming with natural resources. From the coconuts, the natives produced goods like moisturizers, fertilizer, fresh coconut, dried coconut, coconut candy, coconut milk, and fresh coconut juice. All parts of the coconut were used to make many handcrafted items. Even the outer coconut fiber was used to fabricate cushions and building materials.

The next day, our class spent hours observing different Vietnamese corporations. All of the company visits were enriching, but the most memorable was a major tea manufacturing enterprise. This visit left a lasting impression on me because the company's warm welcome and cultural differences were unexpected and rather unique.

Upon arrival to Hung Phat Tea, our class was welcomed with light entertainment and given Asian inspired straw hats as gifts. We all embraced the company's tradition and proudly wore our hats. To me, the gesture symbolized that we were embracing their culture or at least showing some respect. The company played a rhythmic drum beat as a man dressed in an ancient red warrior costume danced and fought a dragon-like character. What I witnessed was fascinating, so I videotaped it and sent the clip to Christophe, hoping he would appreciate the exotic music and theatrical skit. He never responded so I just assumed that he was playing at a gig or practicing his drums in the basement.

Hung Phat Tea welcomed us, fed us, shared their culture, and allowed us to tour their facilities. What stood out most about Hung Phat Tea were the company's culture and its ability to provide free housing to its employees. During the entire visit, their culture of smiling and being happy was a topic of conversation for my cohorts. Maybe it was just foreign to us, as visiting Americans that operate within a predominately capitalist mindset.

Some students thought the presentation was just a marketing campaign. Other students expressed their concerns about the employees' living conditions. Some students left Hung Phat Tea speechless; they didn't know what to make of it. A few students, myself included, viewed the experience as genuine and authentic.

We had only experienced three hours within the company yet, some of the students judged and questioned the company's validity. They wondered whether it was authentic or not. Instead of just living in the moment, some of the students took our views about business and compared that company's practices against what we believe to be appropriate business standards.

For me, the visit to the tea company was a once in a lifetime experience. From a business perspective, they made me feel good. They displayed a happy, positive spirit and they were proud to show off their living quarters for their staff. They had inexpensive labor, but they offered an opportunity for their employees to take care of themselves and their families.

Cambodia

We spent two days in Cambodia. The first day was designated as a free day, so after we checked into the Angkor Wat Victoria Resort, we could do anything; it was considered leisure time. Some of my classmates chose to go shopping while others decided to hang at the swimming pool. I decided to relax and stroll around the hotel premises. I spotted the resort-style salon and spa while exploring the hotel. Curious to learn more about the spa industry in Cambodia, I scheduled a one-hour massage.

My senses were awakened by the fresh scent of eucalyptus upon approaching the spa. The receptionist greeted me with a small plate that had an assortment of fruit and a petite fork. I could hear the chirping of the birds coming from the open-air atrium in the center of the reception area. It was a calm and serene place decorated with warm woods, Asian artifacts, and nature. I took my time eating so that I could stare at each inch of the space to take it all in. The receptionist reached for my plate noticing that I had taken my last bite, then gave me a small cup of warm tea. I finished the tea and proceeded to follow her through a hallway to get to the treatment room. I could hear the faint sound of harp music, which added to the relaxing ambience. When we reached the spa room, the receptionist instructed me to get undressed and to lie down on the massage table underneath the white oversized bath towel that barely hugged the full length of the table. After she exited the treatment room, I removed all my clothes and lay uncomfortably underneath the bath towel. I waited

patiently for the therapist to enter the room. I was hoping
for a person large in stature that could give firm strong
pressure because I prefer deep tissue bodywork. As a
light sound from the spa door creaked, I was greeted by a
young Cambodian lady who was about 4'10" tall and
about 90lbs. Her hair was pulled back in a bun. She wore
no makeup, which was perfectly fine, as she appeared to
be in her late 20s. I had, once again, been paired with a
therapist that did not really do deep tissue massage. I
quickly abandoned the hopes of a deep tissue experience
and decided to close my eyes and make the best of it.
This therapist liked to talk, so I started asking questions
about the requirements to work in the spa. She talked
during the entire massage session. She explained her
experience and rate of pay for working at the five-star
hotel. Then, she went on to tell me about her aspirations
of visiting America. I felt sorry for her after she divulged
the facts about her earnings per year. I continued to
listen to her story until the hour had passed. I didn't
mind listening when she began to share the history of
Angkor Wat and the other temples. I enjoyed learning
about history. The stories were enlightening, and it

inspired me to join my class the next morning to partake in the excursion to the temples.

I was preparing to pay the receptionist twelve dollars for my spa service when the spa manager approached me, introduced herself and asked, "How was your massage?" I responded, "It wasn't bad. I've worked in the spa industry for a while, so instead of relaxing, I tend to overanalyze everything rather than enjoying the treatment." Surprised that we were in the same industry, the manager offered to have coffee with me. I accepted the offer; I could talk spa all day long.

I paid the receptionist, thanked the massage therapist, and give her a small tip. The spa manager and I then walked outside of the spa. We sat at a table near the pool and ordered dark roast coffee. The manager proceeded to tell me her life story. She was French and her husband was from Guadeloupe. I asked her, "How did you end up here in Cambodia if you're from France?" She explained that her husband's friend needed someone to come to Cambodia to manage the spa, so she accepted the contract and started the position over a year ago.

The waiter served us our coffee as we continued to exchange stories. An hour had passed, and we were still talking about spa related issues and discussing the best international skincare brands. We exchanged email addresses after picking each other's brain and agreed that we would keep in touch to share international spa trends. The meeting with the spa manager offered a different perspective. I had never really considered the role of being a consultant to new spa owners or managing a spa within a hotel. After the meeting I thought to myself, "With a master's degree in Business Administration, maybe I too, could manage a high-end spa." I was inspired by meeting the spa manager, so afterwards I decided to call Christophe. Again, Christophe did not answer my call.

The next day, all my classmates were up at 5am boarding the coach that was scheduled to take us to see Angkor Wat at the crack of dawn. Upon arrival at the park, we had to purchase tickets and receive ID badges to enter the historical site. We walked through the ancient ruins and I was struck most by the aggressiveness of the young children selling souvenirs. I saw the Cambodian children's desperation to sell their key chains and other items. I felt moved and was compelled to purchase a few of their souvenirs. The tour guide informed us that the children do attend school, but they are trying to sell their wares to meet basic needs.

By the time the tour of Angkor Wat and Angkor Tom had ended, the weather had warmed up. We walked back to the bus and were delighted to see several elephants. Many people were standing in line for their turn to ride the huge mammal. It was a pleasant sight, yet the thought of riding on the back of an elephant scared me. Instead, I took pictures of the peaceful beast.

Bangkok, Thailand

Bangkok was the final stop on the itinerary. The accommodations at the Peninsula, a sophisticated urban resort, were superb. The five-star hotel offered views of the skyline and access to the Chao Phraya River. Native Thai women, wearing long grey dresses, similar to kimonos, greeted us. Each student registered at the luxurious front desk with passports and credit cards in hand. We all were given two room keys. Bracelets, made of fresh small flowers, were then gently placed around our wrists. The students appreciated the gracious gestures and returned the traditional Thai greeting, "Sawatdee-kah."

Each day in Bangkok was filled with learning about Thailand's history and culture. Our corporate visits included several multinational companies, an independent hospital, and a law firm that focused primarily on protecting intellectual property. We listened to senior executives speak about various topics that ranged from environmental sustainability and how their company was practicing social responsibility, to best business practices and company culture.

Of all company visits, I was most impressed with the independent hospital speaker. He was a retired European doctor who decided to leave his familiar land to start a medical practice in a developing country. He explained, "The first time I visited Thailand, there were no formal hospitals or emergency systems in place. If the locals became sick, they would use traditional remedies or herbs and then wait, hoping to be cured." The doctor continued, "My family and I relocated to this country many years ago. I saw a need in this community that was underserved, so with permission from the Prime Minister, I implemented a system that included access to medical care at an affordable rate. The medical system was not difficult to start. The challenges came with educating the locals about the importance of preventative care and implementing healthy norms. To build the medical practice, we offered unpaid internships. Medical students from all parts of the world could come here to gain hands-on experience with real patients. At the end of the internship, the students had the option to stay in Thailand and practice medicine, or return to their country to continue their studies. It was a win-win situation for all parties involved."

After the corporate visits were over and we returned to the hotel, each student could enjoy the day in their own way. Some of my classmates went shopping for tailor-made suits and custom-designed dresses made of fine linen. Other classmates explored the city, while some chose to relax or dip in the pool.

A group of us decided to be adventurous by going on a bike tour. Three professional cyclists led our cycling excursion. They arrived at our hotel in a ten-passenger coach to transport us to the parking lot located in the back of the Suan Plern Market. We selected the appropriate bike for our size and height then securely attached the protective helmets. I turned on my music, placed my wireless headphones in my ears and departed. The first leg of the journey included peddling a short distance through the city, getting off our bikes, and crossing the river by ferry to get to Bang Kra Jao, a tucked away green oasis.

The fresh air and green jungle scenery of Bang Kra Jao were unexpected. The lush tropical vegetation offered an escape from the city. We cruised peacefully as oncoming vehicles gave us the right of way. Our group chatted as we blazed through the roads surrounded by the tropical landscape. The tour was peaceful. It allowed me to reflect on my life and goals as I grooved to new music by Michael Goldswagger. I peddled up mild hills and pushed myself so hard to complete the journey. I found myself in a thoughtful reflective state once the tour ended. On the way back to the resort, I made a commitment to always make time for myself.

This time in Thailand afforded me space to regroup, recharge and clear my mind. The bike tour was an awesome challenge that was fun and rewarding. I promised myself that I would definitely do more outdoor activities when I returned home to the states. The floating market and bike tour were the best experiences while in Thailand.

The Final Note:

By the time the international residency was over, and each student made plans to go back to the states, Sydney was so proud of herself. She could not believe the accomplishments that she had just achieved. She reflected on her past and remembered a time when she was once a college dropout, a divorcee and single parent struggling to provide the basic necessities for her children. She was a product of a broken home, daughter of a drug addict, and survivor of domestic violence, yet now, she could look in the mirror, head held high. With her faith firmly planted in God, she was convinced that she could do anything that she put her mind to, despite insecurities about her past. The experience in Asia gave her time to learn about herself and provided her the opportunity to gain a broader outlook on different cultures and different business practices.

Sydney was grateful for all that she had learned, yet she was ready to go back home to be with Christophe and her children. She missed being with her husband and seeing the smiles on her children's faces. Going over to Asia made her appreciate her family and their time apart caused her to never again want to spend another day away from them.

When she arrived home, everything was peaceful, exactly as it was when she had departed on her Southeast Asia journey. Christophe's smile and deep-set dimples drew her near, while her children innocently laughed and embraced her tightly. With anticipation in their eyes, they all waited to hear the tales of a foreign land. Sydney, like her grandma Nadeya, painted vivid pictures in her children's imagination. She shared foreign experiences and Asian artifacts, which inspired her children and Christophe.

Sydney spent hours telling stories and answering questions then prayed over her children. After recalling the events of her journey, she embraced her children, wished them a goodnight, then made her way to her bedroom. She had been looking forward to some alone time with Christophe. Sydney removed all of her clothes, showered, and slipped into a white-laced negligée then laid across her bed to entice her husband. Upon entering the room, Christophe took a moment to gaze at his wife as he missed her dearly. Desire could be seen in his eyes as he immediately removed her lingerie. Sydney and Christophe both exhaled, "Thank you, God."

Patiently, I waited for Christophe to turn me on, but he never did. He chose to love his wife in silence, with only her breath in his ear and her heartbeat on his. Without a single thought about me, hours pass by as he overindulges in his wife. I have never been the jealous type, but I must admit that this was the first time I've felt betrayed by him. Throughout the course of this relationship, I have fought for my position in Christophe's heart. I was his first love. I was the one who ignited the passion in him. I brought him through the hard times; I've been a subliminal influence in his life. However, while Sydney was away, I felt a shift in

Christophe. He reflected on his relationship with Sydney and committed to making more time for her and their marriage. So, upon Sydney's return, I decided to relinquish my pull to be his most dominant thought. It's unquestionable that the joy and harmony he shares with Sydney has more rhythm than any song I could ever sing.

P.S.- Sydney, I concede, for now.

Chapter 10: Asia Bound

NOTE FROM THE EDITOR

Bravo! What an encore performance from Alicia Hilaire. *Notes from the Mistress* is a love story that elegantly captures some of marriages common issues surrounding spousal prioritization, self-preservation, and core value alignment. It was easy to adore both main characters as their personalities unfolded at home and abroad. The music's personification in the notes, at the beginning of each chapter, was a unique touch that gave a voice to an unseen challenge within the couple's marriage. I highly recommend listening to the songs mentioned within the story as you read the book. The lyrics will add a whole mood to your reading enjoyment. If you have ever experienced relationship, I'm sure that you will fall head over heels in love with this story. Way to go Alicia!

Cheers!!

Kelly Cook

ABOUT THE AUTHOR

Alicia Hilaire is the owner and operator of Suwanee Georgia's premier boutique spa and salon, Spa Li Cia. Alicia has a bachelor's degree from the Art Institute of Atlanta and a MBA degree from Georgia State University. She is currently studying to earn a post bachelorette degree in French. *Sydney's Bleu* is her debut novel, and *Notes from the Mistress* is the sequel. Alicia is a francophone enthusiast. She enjoys traveling to new and interesting cities around the world. She lives in Suwanee, Georgia with her husband and children.